UNDERSTANDING
WALTER MOSLEY

UNDERSTANDING CONTEMPORARY AMERICAN LITERATURE
Matthew J. Bruccoli, Founding Editor
Linda Wagner-Martin, Series Editor

Volumes on

Edward Albee | Sherman Alexie | Nelson Algren
Paul Auster | Nicholson Baker | John Barth | Donald Barthelme
The Beats | Thomas Berger | The Black Mountain Poets | Robert Bly
T. C. Boyle | Truman Capote | Raymond Carver | Michael Chabon
Fred Chappell | Chicano Literature | Contemporary American Drama
Contemporary American Horror Fiction | Contemporary American Literary Theory
Contemporary American Science Fiction, 1926–1970 | Contemporary American
Science Fiction, 1970–2000 | Contemporary Chicana Literature | Robert Coover
Philip K. Dick | James Dickey | E. L. Doctorow | Rita Dove | Don DeLillo | Dave Eggers
Louise Erdrich | John Gardner | George Garrett | Tim Gautreaux | William Gibson
John Hawkes | Joseph Heller | Lillian Hellman | Beth Henley | James Leo Herlihy
David Henry Hwang | John Irving | Randall Jarrell | Charles Johnson | Diane Johnson
Edward P. Jones | Adrienne Kennedy | William Kennedy | Jack Kerouac | Jamaica Kincaid
Etheridge Knight | Tony Kushner | Ursula K. Le Guin | Jonathan Lethem
Denise Levertov | Bernard Malamud | David Mamet | Bobbie Ann Mason
Colum McCann | Cormac McCarthy | Jill McCorkle | Carson McCullers
W. S. Merwin | Arthur Miller | Steven Millhauser | Lorrie Moore
Toni Morrison's Fiction | Walter Mosley | Vladimir Nabokov | Gloria Naylor
Joyce Carol Oates | Tim O'Brien Flannery O'Connor | Cynthia Ozick
Chuck Palahniuk | Suzan-Lori Parks| Walker Percy | Katherine Anne Porter
Richard Powers | Reynolds Price | Annie Proulx | Thomas Pynchon | Theodore Roethke
Philip Roth | Richard Russo | May Sarton Hubert Selby, Jr. | Mary Lee Settle
Sam Shepard | Neil Simon | Isaac Bashevis Singer | Jane Smiley | Gary Snyder
William Stafford | Robert Stone | Anne Tyler | Gerald Vizenor | Kurt Vonnegut
David Foster Wallace | Robert Penn Warren | James Welch | Eudora Welty
Colson Whitehead | Tennessee Williams | August Wilson | Charles Wright

UNDERSTANDING

WALTER MOSLEY

Jennifer Larson

The University of South Carolina Press

Published by the University of South Carolina Press
Columbia, South Carolina 29208

www.sc.edu/uscpress

Manufactured in the United States of America

24 23 22 21 20 19 18 17 16   10 9 8 7 6 5 4 3 2 1

Library of Congress Cataloging-in-Publication Data
can be found at http://catalog.loc.gov/.

ISBN: 978-1-61117-701-5 (hardcover)
ISBN: 978-1-61117-702-2 (ebook)

This book was printed on a recycled paper with
30 percent postconsumer waste content.

CONTENTS

SERIES EDITOR'S PREFACE

The Understanding Contemporary American Literature series was founded by the estimable Matthew J. Bruccoli (1931–2008), who envisioned these volumes as guides or companions for students as well as good nonacademic readers, a legacy that will continue as new volumes are developed to fill in gaps among the nearly one hundred series volumes published to date and to embrace a host of new writers only now making their marks on our literature.

As Professor Bruccoli explained in his preface to the volumes he edited, because much influential contemporary literature makes special demands, "the word understanding in the titles was chosen deliberately. Many willing readers lack an adequate understanding of how contemporary literature works; that is, of what the author is attempting to express and the means by which it is conveyed." Aimed at fostering this understanding of good literature and good writers, the criticism and analysis in the series provide instruction in how to read certain contemporary writers—explicating their material, language, structures, themes, and perspectives— and facilitate a more profitable experience of the works under discussion.

In the twenty-first century Professor Bruccoli's prescience gives us an avenue to publish expert critiques of significant contemporary American writing. The series continues to map the literary landscape and to provide both instruction and enjoyment. Future volumes will seek to introduce new voices alongside canonized favorites, to chronicle the changing literature of our times, and to remain, as Professor Bruccoli conceived, contemporary in the best sense of the word.

Linda Wagner-Martin, Series Editor

ACKNOWLEDGMENTS

Special thanks, as always, to my long-time mentors, Dr. Sandra Govan and Dr. Trudier Harris, as well as to my friends and family—especially Doug and Colin—for their constant support and encouragement. Also, a nod to Tim Davis, who gave me my first Walter Mosley book fifteen years ago.

CHAPTER ONE

Understanding Walter Mosley

Since Walter Mosley began his writing career with a series of immensely popular mystery novels, readers may be surprised to hear that he is "arguably the most prolific novelist of the late twentieth and early twenty-first centuries,"[1] publishing across genres, including—but not limited to—nonfiction, science fiction, drama, and even young adult fiction. All of these texts, though, feature Mosley's trademark accessibility as well as his penchant for creating narratives that both entertain and instruct.

Mosley was born January 12, 1952, and raised in Los Angeles (the setting for most of his fiction)—first South Central, then West Los Angeles. His mother, Ella, was a Jewish school administrator; his father, Leroy, was an African American school custodian. Their marriage was a happy one, and neither Ella's nor Leroy's family was hostile about the interracial union. Both of Mosley's parents encouraged his early love of reading, and his father, in particular, played a key role in shaping his view on race, community, and history. Variations on Leroy Mosley's stories—especially his stories about his own father and childhood—reappear frequently in Walter Mosley's fiction and nonfiction. And although he did not become a professional writer until he was in his thirties, Mosley looks back to a favorite high-school English teacher and a love of comic books as initially inspiring his interest in writing.[2]

Mosley attended Goddard College in Vermont, but he felt more compelled to wander—by hitchhiking around the country—than study, so he dropped out of Goddard. After working in a variety of jobs, such as a potter and a caterer, he eventually returned to college at Johnson State College, also in Vermont, and graduated with a political science degree in 1977. From there, he went on to begin graduate studies at the University of Massachusetts while working as a computer programmer in Boston. He felt uninspired by these studies, however, and decided to move to New York City in 1981.[3]

While still supporting himself as a programmer, Mosley read Alice Walker's *The Color Purple*. He was moved by the language of this novel and was inspired to try writing his own novel. His inner writer discovered, Mosley enrolled in the City College at the City University of New York's (CUNY) Creative Writing Program in 1985. There, he studied fiction writing with Frederick Tuten and poetry writing with Bill Matthews. During these studies, he wrote the manuscript for *Gone Fishin'* and in the late 1980s tried unsuccessfully to publish it.[4] With *Gone Fishin'*, Mosley was hoping to create a series of stories based on experiences, like his father's, of migration from the deep South. No publisher, however, saw Mosley's works as "marketable" until he reworked them as mysteries.[5]

Mosley was inspired to revise parts of *Gone Fishin'* into what would become the first Easy Rawlins mystery, *Devil in a Blue Dress*, after reading Graham Greene's screenplay for the 1949 film *The Third Man*. Under the tutelage of Tuten, as well as his other CUNY mentors, Bill Matthews and Edna O'Brien, Mosley created a novel so impressive that Tuten took it to his own agent, Gloria Loomis. Loomis secured Mosley a contract with Norton to publish not only *Devil*, but also two additional novels.[6]

This contract officially launched what would become one of American literature's most prolific writing careers. In his first decade of professional writing, Mosley averaged a book a year.[7] In 2013–14 alone, he released four new books and produced a play. The tough and cool Ezekiel "Easy" Rawlins would become the hero of over a dozen more books in two decades following *Devil*'s release. In the years between Easy Rawlins stories, Mosley would produce three additional series, four science-fiction texts (one for young adults), two works of erotica, a play, a graphic novel, three sets of short stories, five nonfiction books, and seven additional novels—for a total over three dozen (and counting) works.

Mosley has won, among other honors, an O'Henry Award in 1996, an Anisfield-Wolf Book Award in 1998, a Grammy Award in 2001 for his liner notes to Richard Pryor's *And It's Deep Too*, the 2004 Pen Center Lifetime Achievement Award, and the NAACP Image Award for Outstanding Literary Work in Fiction in 2007 and 2009. Mosley's work received increased popular and critical attention in 1992 when soon-to-be-elected-president Bill Clinton carried *Devil in a Blue Dress* to campaign stops and listed Mosley as one of his favorite writers.[8] Since then, with only a few exceptions, Mosley's works have continued to achieve both popular and critical success.

In addition, four of Mosley's works have been adapted for the screen. Most notably, the 1995 feature-film adaptation of *Devil in a Blue Dress* stars Denzel Washington, and the 1998 television adaptation of *Always Outnumbered, Always Outgunned* (with the shortened title *Always Outnumbered*), stars Academy Award nominee Laurence Fishburne. These adaptations are further testament to the diversity, versatility, and mass appeal of Mosley's works.

The works achieve this appeal by offering a thematic or cultural entry point for almost any type of reader. Yet, in so doing, Mosley does not "water down" key conflicts, especially key racial conflicts. Mosley makes racial dynamics and histories such an authentic and realistic element of his stories that both black and white audiences feel not only comfortable with, but also consistently drawn to, his characters' narratives. At the same time, these narratives pay homage to and/or engage some of the African American literary and cultural traditions' most dynamic tropes and characters—such as the blues/jazz aesthetic, folklore, slavery/freedom, Langston Hughes's Jesse B. Semple, Ralph Ellison's enigmatic protagonist in *Invisible Man,* and even the hyper-masculine blaxploitation hero-detective Shaft. Connecting to such rich and provocative traditions suggests that Mosley's works are simultaneously artistic and political. Indeed, Mosley has recently reflected, "One of the interesting things you find about writing fiction is that any fiction you write has to be political[. . . .] If you write about black people, you write about white men[. . . .] it has to be political."[9]

The diversity of his corpus means that Mosley receives praise from a diverse group of readers and popular critics who often cite their appreciation for his treatment of race as an element that is essential to his characters' identities but not to every aspect of their stories; race remains ever dynamic and personal for these characters and their narratives. Mosley navigates the often-treacherous landscape of identity politics by asking audiences to connect with the characters' racial, cultural, and social realities through—rather than in addition to—engagement with the narrative.

The Easy Rawlins texts in particular offer a unique perspective on race, class, and masculinity in the mid-twentieth century. *Devil in a Blue Dress* is set in 1948 Watts. Most of the remaining texts gradually move Easy twenty years forward through the tumultuous decades of the civil rights movement, while *Gone Fishin'* looks back nearly ten years to examine key events that shaped Easy and his friend/sidekick, Mouse. Easy therefore represents a matrix of history, narrative, and identity that is just as enigmatic as the mysteries he solves. Fearless Jones and Paris Minton share Easy's 1950s Los Angeles context in *Fearless Jones* (2001) and its sequels, but approach their conflicts from a darker, more violent perspective. Paris, the sheepish bookstore owner, and Fearless, the veteran and ex-con, even interact with Easy in two of his novels. When Mosley shifts the focus of his mysteries to twenty-first-century New York City in the Leonid McGill stories, he carefully considers the impact of twenty-first-century discourse about race and ethnicity on the mystery genre.

Mosley's science fiction and erotica also explore the relationship between genre and race. In "Black to the Future," his essay on science fiction, Mosley writes, "Science fiction allows history to be rewritten or ignored. Science fiction promises a future full of possibility, alternative lives, and even regret. . . . Through science fiction you can have a black president, a black world, or simply a say in the way things are."[10] So, novels such as *Blue Light* envision a reality in which race is not a source of alienation, but of community and redemption. Similarly, hyper-sensual *Diablerie* imagines sex as a vehicle for self-awareness that contributes to a deeper understanding of racial identity.

Even without the label of a specific genre, Mosley's other works—especially his Socrates Fortlow books and the enigmatic novel *The Man in My Basement*—challenge readers to explore the philosophical debates that inform not only discourses of race, but also of morality in general. Many of these debates are then explored in more detail and applied to modern politics in Mosley's nonfiction texts—*Workin' on the Chain Gang: Shaking off the Dead Hand of History* (2000), *What Next: An African American Initiative Toward World Peace* (2003), *Life Out of Context: Which Includes a Proposal for the Non-violent Takeover of the House of Representatives* (2006), and *Twelve Steps Toward Political Revelation* (2011).

The mystery novels, though, receive most of the public's praise and scholars' attention. The first book-length study of Mosley's work, Charles E. Wilson's *Walter Mosley: A Critical Companion* (2003), covers eight novels—four Easy Rawlins mysteries, the blues novel *RL's Dream* (1995), *Always Outnumbered, Always Outgunned* (1998), and *Fearless Jones*—in detail, and the other Easy Rawlins mysteries, science fiction, and sequels published at the time are covered in context with their related texts. However, Wilson notes that, "because *Futureland* and *The Tempest Tales* are collections of stories rather than whole novels, a full discussion of them is not merited."[11]

The next and most recent book of criticism is a 2008 essay collection, *Finding A Way Home: A Critical Assessment of Walter Mosley's Fiction*, which features essays interrogating nearly every aspect of Mosley's corpus. Editors Owen E. Brady and Derek C. Maus also include an overview of the texts Mosley published in the time frame it took them to commission, compile, and release the collection, noting, "Time and Walter Mosley wait for no critics, a fact that greatly complicates the task of presenting a thorough overview of his work"—a complication that also applies to the present study.[12]

Indeed, Mosley's corpus is too vast and is expanding too quickly to be covered exhaustively in any single volume. *Understanding Walter Mosley* will therefore cover representative works from each of Mosley's series, thematic threading linking the genre and non-genre fictions, and the connections among Mosley's fiction and nonfiction texts. In all cases—with the exception of the Easy Rawlins novels—there is little existing critical conversation on the texts to explore.

Although a handful of literary critics have penned articles—most of which appear in the book-length studies noted above—on *The Man in My Basement* and *Always Outnumbered, Always Outgunned,* academic analysis on Mosley focuses almost exclusively on Easy Rawlins in general and on *Devil in a Blue Dress* in particular, and his aesthetic in these texts has been compared to both Raymond Chandler's and Chester Himes's, despite Mosley's efforts to create literary space for himself.[13] For Mosley, though, the mystery genre is merely a lens through which readers can understand relevant social and political questions, past and present. He explains, "Mysteries, stories about crime, about detectives, are the ones that really ask the existentialist questions, [. . .] such as 'How do I act in an imperfect world when I want to be perfect?' I'm not really into clues and that sort of thing, although I do put them in my stories. I like the moral questions."[14]

While Mosley's nonfiction texts seem to engage larger social questions most directly, all of Mosley's texts, regardless of genre, might be read as treatises on race, class, gender, politics, history, and even the act of writing. Again, however, Mosley himself complicates this connection by rejecting the notion of an overt unifying principle or theme among his works. He explains in *Life Out of Context,* "[. . .] when I thought about my own work—which ranges from crime stories to short stories to so-called literary fiction to science fiction to works like the one you're reading here—I can hardly find a context between one book and the next."[15]

However, scholars' lack of attention to Mosley's nonfiction, as well as much of his non-mystery work, leads to an intriguing bifurcation of his oeuvre that creates safe, if not sacred, spaces for both "scholarly" and "popular" audiences. Students of American literature might read *Devil in a Blue Dress* in their courses, and through this text and scholarship on it, those new to Mosley can walk away with valuable insights about black masculinity, black history, and racial politics. They will also realize, just from this cursory introduction, that there are, in fact, black genre fiction writers.

Those readers who care to get to know Mosley a little better, though, become part of a devoted group who love Mosley and his heroes for better or worse. Those who have read only *Devil in a Blue Dress,* though, do not know that Easy's character gets a little more complicated as his series moves on: he kills, womanizes, drinks, and even dies. Mosley's other novels feature a wide range of formerly and currently nefarious characters, including the murderer and rapist Socrates Fortlow in *Always Outnumbered, Always Outgunned* and the morally void Ben Dibbuk in *Diablerie*. Paris Minton initially leaves his best friend to rot in jail in *Fearless Jones*, and Leonid McGill constantly cheats on his wife. But all of these characters nevertheless eventually find redemption and community in their texts, revealing the impressive resilience of human nature and making them "likable" to readers.

Reading more Mosley, especially the personal narratives, can make readers feel like they are getting to know a friend. So, when that friend walks into a crowded reading, the readers are really excited to see him. The scholars have one Mosley, and that's valuable, but there is another Mosley for everyone else— a cool, approachable guy who comments on fans' Facebook posts and hugs bookstore owners.

Mosley has also cultivated an image of himself as a prolific writer and engaged public intellectual. The latter persona is a second key element of Mosley's popularity. The seemingly never-ending conversation about Nicholas Kristof's now infamous *New York Times* article, "Professors, We Need You!" points to American's fascination with and craving for a public intellectual. Kristof's article points to academia's failure to give this monolithic figure to the world as most academics "cloister themselves like medieval monks" rather than selflessly give their time and knowledge to the world.[16]

Mosley, though, stays visible and available. The "appearances" section of his Web site (www.waltermosley.com), for example, often features a schedule that has Mosley in cities across the country, giving multiple readings even in a single week. At an independent bookstore event in Raleigh, North Carolina, the relatively large shop had a standing-room crowd almost an hour before Mosley's scheduled arrival, and the very diverse (by every demographic account) audience was abuzz with anticipation. When Mosley walked in and made his way through the crowd, an air of almost giddy excitement fell over the room. And while Mosley does read from his works at these appearances, he spends time just talking as well: mostly about politics, some about writing, and just a little about Easy Rawlins.

Mosley also maintains an active social media presence on Facebook. There he posts information about book releases and appearance, articles about him and his works, and links to other pages or events that interest him. He also hosts reader question-and-answer sessions there during which fans can post comments during a specific hour, and Mosley will comment back—sometimes extensively. During a September 2014 session, for example, fans asked questions about the writing process, about when the next Leonid McGill novel would come out (May 2015), about whether Don Cheadle portrayed Mouse as he'd imagined ("better"), about when he was coming to town for a visit, and about his decision to bring Easy back to life ("I woke up one day, and Easy was waiting").

Mosley's popularity endures because Mosley endures—he just keeps writing more texts: more fiction, more nonfiction, and, of course, more Easy Rawlins, even when that meant literally resurrecting the hero. And Mosley not only writes but also talks and writes about writing—its joys, its pains, and its value. Mosley's nonfiction allows readers unprecedented glimpses into his creative process, thereby removing the "mystery" of the writing process and making himself and his craft more accessible for his audiences.

Mosley dedicates an entire book, *This Year You Write Your Novel*, to explaining his process and encouraging readers to not only talk about his or others' writing, but also to write themselves. He believes that "any manager, mother, counselor, teacher, or guy who hangs out on the corner telling tall tales is a writer-in-waiting," so Mosley wants to show his readers "how you can direct your natural abilities at communication into creative prose" (3).[17] This process, he warns, will not always be easy or painless, and he details how, even more than twenty years into his career, "after publishing more than twenty-seven books and at least as many short stories, I still get rejected on a regular basis" (101). However, the writing process, he reassures, "will transform you. It will give you confidence, pleasure, a deeper understanding of how you think and feel; it will make you into an artist and a fledgling craftsperson[. . . .] maybe it will do more" (103).

Mosley's openness about his writing, his dedication to this craft, and his continued commitment to satisfying his readers' hunger for more of his texts mean that Mosley's work is not a monologue; it is a conversation. Writing in general, and Mosley's writing in particular, then, is not an abstract, aloof discourse, but rather a vehicle for mutual understanding and tangible social transformation.

CHAPTER TWO

Easy's Evolution
Relationships, Race, and Genre

Although just under six-foot-one and 185 pounds (190 at Christmas, he says), Ezekiel Porterhouse Rawlins is—at least for many of his fans—larger than life. His stories are not just thrillers, but also, Walter Mosley says, they explore "the black migration from the Deep South to Los Angeles and this blue-collar existential hero moving through time."[1] The hero's quest begins in 1948 Watts, Los Angeles, and gradually moves Easy twenty years forward through the tumultuous decades of the civil rights movement. While on this journey, Easy offers his unique perspective on race, class, masculinity, and many other issues pertinent to his life and community. And he comes, through this perspective, to represent a matrix of history, narrative, and identity that is just as enigmatic as the mysteries he solves.

Among all the works in Mosley's impressive corpus, the Easy Rawlins texts are, by far, the most critically accepted and receive, by far, the most critical attention. The first five novels in particular have been interrogated at length by both academic and popular critics. In such an expansive and still-expanding set of narratives, though, considering trends that run throughout the entire series helps chart Easy's evolution—as a man and as a detective—as well as his narrative's evolution within and beyond crime-fiction conventions. Easy's individual growth and change are most evident in his long-term relationships and in his observations about race. These personal developments also then shape his detective work and the mysteries that define his narratives.

This evolution can be charted through the eleven mysteries that feature Easy Rawlins as well as the prequel, *Gone Fishin'*, and the short mysteries in *Six Easy Pieces*. The first five texts are less tangled narratives—by nature of the fewer recurring characters and less need for backstories about previous texts—and most have been treated at length elsewhere, most notably in Charles E. Wilson's *Walter Mosley: A Critical Companion* (2003).

Through the course of Mosley's texts, Easy's relationships with his friends and with the women in his life change, as do his perspectives on race. Easy observes how race in America has changed from the 1940s to the 1960s. Tracing this evolution paves the way for a greater understanding of where Easy Rawlins fits in the mystery fiction tradition.

The Stories

In *Devil in a Blue Dress* (1990; dedicated to Mosley's ex-wife Joy Kellman, mentor Frederic Tuten, and father, Leroy Mosley), set in 1948, Easy has just lost his job at the Champion Aircraft assembly factory and is desperate to find work so he can pay the mortgage on his beloved small house. His bartender friend, ex-boxer Joppy, introduces Easy to DeWitt Albright, who hires Easy to find Daphne Monet, the love interest of Albright's very wealthy client Todd Carter. As soon as Easy gets information about Monet from his friend Coretta, Coretta is murdered. Easy immediately becomes the police's prime suspect and must stay on the case to clear his name—especially as more of his acquaintances turn up dead and Albright and others threaten his life.

Easy soon learns that many of his friends have lied to him about their motives and identities. He is also drawn to Monet, and the two have an affair. Easy's long-time, bloodthirsty associate Mouse arrives in town just in time to save Easy's life and offers to help with the case. When Mouse sees Monet, he recognizes that she is actually his old acquaintance Ruby Hanks, who is passing for white. Daphne stole thirty thousand dollars to flee town with her brother Frank Green after blackmailers revealed her true identity to Carter. Albright and Joppy kidnap Daphne, and when Mouse and Easy come to save her, Mouse kills both men, as well as Frank Green. Daphne, Easy, and Mouse divide the money, which Easy invests in real estate.

In *A Red Death: An Easy Rawlins Mystery* (1991; "*Dedicated to the memory of* Alberta Jackson and Lillian Keller *with special thanks to* Daniel and Elizabeth Russell"), set in 1953 (during the Red Scare), Easy has purchased multiple properties through a dummy corporation, and the IRS is investigating him for tax fraud/evasion. In an effort to avoid harassment by the overzealous IRS agent Reginald Lawrence, Easy makes a deal with agent Craxton, who offers to let Easy avoid jail and repay his debt over time if Easy helps him spy on Chaim Wenzler, a Jewish communist who is organizing poverty relief efforts at First African Baptist Church.

Easy eventually discovers that Wenzler helped one of Easy's former coworkers from Champion Aircraft hide stolen defense design plans. He also discovers that Lawrence murdered Wenzler, Reverend Towne (the First African Baptist's minister), and one of Easy's tenants (Poinsettia) to cover up his own tax-fraud scheme. Meanwhile, Mouse's estranged wife EttaMae comes to Los Angeles, and she and Easy begin an affair. Easy is in love with Etta, but after Mouse shows renewed interest in his son, EttaMae goes back to him.

In *White Butterfly: An Easy Rawlins Mystery* (1992; dedicated to Leroy Mosley, "for the stories he keeps on telling"), set in 1956, the Los Angeles Police Department strong-arms Easy into helping them find a serial killer who previously was killing only black prostitutes, but has suddenly switched to a white victim, Robin Garnett. Easy discovers that Robin had been living as prostitute Cyndi Starr in a Watts brothel for months before her death, and he even tracks down the serial killer. However, Easy becomes convinced that the man, whom the police promptly murder, is not actually Cyndi's killer. This conviction intensifies when Easy discovers that Cyndi had a baby who she hid with friends.

With the help of Cyndi's seemingly devoted, grieving parents, Easy tries to find the child and Cyndi's killer; however, he realizes that Cyndi's father, powerful prosecutor Vernon Garnett, killed his daughter to avoid public embarrassment. Garnett has Easy jailed for extortion so Garnett can destroy any evidence and murder any witnesses who can implicate him in his daughter's killing. Mouse, however, thwarts this plan by bailing Easy out and helping him track Vernon down. As the case comes together, though, Easy's personal life unravels. Easy's wife, Regina, alienated by Easy's secret real estate dealings and questionable friends, leaves Easy for Dupree, and takes their infant daughter, Edna, with her. Easy keeps himself together, though, by focusing on caring for his son, Jesus, and his new ward, Cyndi Starr's infant daughter, Feather, who the police presumed to be dead.

In *Black Betty: An Easy Rawlins Mystery* (1994; dedicated to Leroy Mosley, "who died on New Years Day, 1993"), set in 1961, Easy lives job to job, struggling as a single father. His financial investments are tied up and threatened by a large white developer, so he feels compelled to take on the job of finding Elizabeth Eady (also known as Black Betty), a childhood crush who mysteriously fled the white household where she lived and worked. Easy locates Betty's brother Marlon's home, but there he finds only pieces of Marlon and a check that leads him to Sarah Cain, the matriarch in the household that employed Betty. His dealings with the Cains eventually reveal that Betty had secret children with Albery Cain, the family's brutal patriarch, and that Cain may have left his entire fortune to Betty. So Easy believes someone close to the remaining Cain family is trying to kill off Betty and her children in the hope of restoring the fortune to the white heirs.

Easy and private investigator Saul Lynx discover that Sarah Cain's ex-husband, Ronald, is the plan's mastermind, but not before he has murdered both of Betty's children and thus emotionally destroyed Betty. At the same time, Easy worries over Mouse's revenge quest for the man that fingered him for the murder of Bruno Ingram, and Easy struggles emotionally as he watches his old friend Martin waste away from terminal illness. While investigating Betty's case, Easy often diverts his attention to finding Mouse's actual snitch. Easy instead tells Mouse, though, that Martin turned him in, in order to give Martin the mercy killing he desperately wants.

In *A Little Yellow Dog: An Easy Rawlins Mystery* (1996; no dedication, only the note, "it was the dog's fault"), set in 1963, Easy has been working for two years as the head custodian at Sojourner Truth Junior High School. This quiet life suddenly gets more complicated, however, when he has sex with a teacher, Idabell Turner. Ida's brother-in-law, Roman Gateau, turns up dead on the school grounds soon after. Idabell then disappears, leaving her little yellow dog, Pharaoh, in Easy's care. The cops suspect Easy is involved in the murder, so he begins investigating Roman's murder and Idabell's disappearance, and he finds Roman's twin brother and Idabell's husband, Holland, also murdered. Easy soon finds himself caught up in an elaborate web of sex, drugs, larceny, and blackmail that involves everyone from low-level gangsters to high-level school administrators. Idabell resurfaces from hiding, tells him the backstory about Holland's drug use and anger issues, and asks him to help her get her affairs in order before she leaves the country. In particular, she asks Easy to leave a letter for her friend Bonnie Shay, a flight attendant.

When Easy returns, he finds that Idabell has also been murdered, so he seeks out Bonnie, who eventually reveals the Gasteau brothers' smuggling operation and the roles that the brothers violently forced her and Idabell to play in that operation. Easy questions more of the brothers' associates and figures out that Holland killed Roman, primarily out of jealousy, and that Bonnie killed Holland. When he asks her about the murder, she explains that she killed him in self-defense after he raped her. Meanwhile, Jackson Blue comes to Easy for help because gangsters have put a bounty on him for encroaching on their numbers business. Easy works out a trade with mob boss Philly Stetz: Jackson will hand over the "bookie box" answering machines that have been making his business so successful, Easy will had over the drugs Bonnie has from her last smuggling run, and the mob—in turn—will leave Jackson and Bonnie alone. Two of Stetz's men go rogue and ambush Easy and Mouse before the trade. Mouse is shot, and appears to die.

In *Gone Fishin': An Easy Rawlins Novel* (1997; dedicated to Mosley's mother, Ella) a non-mystery prequel to the Easy Rawlins series, Easy is in his late teens and is living in 1930s Houston. Mouse has just become engaged to EttaMae, and Easy and Mouse travel to Pariah, Mouse's hometown, so Mouse can confront his abusive and purportedly wealthy stepfather, Daddy Reese, and demand money from him. On the way down, Mouse and Easy pick up two hitchhikers, Clifton and Ernestine, who are on the run after Clifton killed a man in a bar fight over Ernestine. The group heads to the home of Momma Jo, a voodoo witch living in the swampland outside of Pariah with her disfigured son, Domaque (Dom).

Jo not only agrees to hide the couple, but she also gives them a love potion to help them improve their physical connection. Easy also drinks the potion and has an intense sexual encounter with Jo. Afterward, Dom and Mouse take Easy fishing, and then they visit Reese, who threatens them after Mouse kills Reese's dogs. Meanwhile Easy has become ill, so Mouse leaves him under the care of Dom's rich white benefactor and teacher, Miss Dixon, the town matriarch. Dom then takes Easy to stay with Miss Alexander, Mouse's aunt.

While convalescing at Miss Alexander's store, Easy discovers more about Mouse's past and decides that he wants to learn how to read. He also has flashbacks to the last night he saw his father. When Easy sees Reese again at church in Pariah, the hard, angry man is gaunt and weak—a victim of Jo's voodoo. Easy's illness worsens as well, but Jo heals him. With renewed strength, Easy goes into the woods to look for Mouse, who he suspects is headed to Reese's house. When Easy arrives there, he finds Clifton trying to convince Mouse to release Reese from the basket Mouse has stuffed him in and is violently kicking. The basket pops open and Reese attacks Clifton, wrestling his gun from him and shooting him. Easy tackles Reese and loses consciousness. When he wakes up to Mouse's shouts, Reese and Clifton are dead. When they return to Houston, Easy becomes reclusive and agrees to attend Mouse's wedding only after Etta's entreaties. Easy then decides to move to California, where he can start a new life with the safety that comes from anonymity.

In *Bad Boy Brawley Brown: An Easy Rawlins Novel* (2001; dedicated to Leroy Mosley), set in 1964, Easy is struggling with accepting the reality of and overcoming his guilt over Mouse's death. Looking for a distraction, Easy agrees to help his friend John's girlfriend, Alva Torres, find her estranged son, Brawley. Brawley has become involved with a group of black militants called the Urban Revolutionary Party, who are on the verge of transitioning from political rhetoric to armed insurrection. Easy begins his investigation by visiting the home of Alva's cousin and Brawley's former guardian, Isolda Moore. Instead of finding Isolda, though, Easy finds Brawley's father, Aldridge Brown, dead. Easy then attends one of the Urban Revolutionary Party's meetings, and he sees Brawley across the room just before the police raid the meeting. Easy tracks down

Isolda, who tells Easy about Brawley's violent relationship with his father and that she fears Brawley killed Aldridge.

Anxious to find Brawley before the police do, Easy follows Brawley's girl-friend, Clarissa, and she leads him to the missing young man, who runs out before Easy can talk to him. The police, with photos of Easy at the party meeting, approach Easy to demand his help in thwarting the group's plans for an armed attack. Fearing the repercussions of refusing, Easy agrees to keep them informed on the progress of his investigation, which next leads him to Brawley's high-school girlfriend, BobbiAnne Terrell, who is keeping a stockpile of weapons for a splinter group of the Urban Revolutionary Party. The group's leader, Anton Breland, claims that they are just going to move the guns for cash, not use them for an insurrection, but when the movement's patriarch, Henry Strong, is murdered, and Brawley's friend—the "reformed" thief Mercury—disappears, Easy realizes that Brawley is in more serious trouble that Alva and John realized.

Easy also figures out that Strong was a double-agent who was spying on the Urban Revolutionary Party, and he tracks the splinter group to a rental house, where he discovers plans for an elaborate armored-car payroll robbery as well as evidence that Strong was sleeping with Isolda. When Easy confronts Isolda, she admits to betraying Strong to Mercury, who also killed Aldridge, and she gives Easy more details about the robbery. Determined to keep his promise to Alva that he would bring Brawley home safely, Easy sets up a pretend police ambush to draw out the robbers, and he shoots Brawley in the leg. Undeterred by Brawley's injuries, the group continues with the heist, during which all the members are killed by the actual police.

Six Easy Pieces: Easy Rawlins Stories (2002–3; dedicated to screenwriter/producer Walter Bernstein) is a collection of short stories about Easy's investigations immediately following *Bad Boy Brawley Brown*. The stories were each published separately in the 2002 Washington Square Press paperback editions of the first six Easy Rawlins novels and compiled into a single edition in 2003. The volume borrows its title from the lauded scientist Richard Feynman's 1994 collection of published lectures, *Six Easy Pieces: Essentials of Physics Explained by Its Most Brilliant Teacher,* and accordingly it offers "essential" keys to Easy's life and character—past, present, and future.

The first story, "Smoke," resolves Easy's conflict with his boss, Principal Hiram Newgate, after a mysterious arson attempt at Sojourner Truth Junior High. Then, in "Crimson Stain," Easy follows a lead suggesting that Mouse is still alive, but when that lead takes him to a dead young woman instead, he brings her killer to justice. In the next story, "Silver Lining," Easy saves his business partner, Jewell, from her greedy family, and in "Lavender," Mouse's widow,

Etta, resurfaces to ask for help finding and protecting a young black musician who has run off with a white heiress. Saul Lynx returns in "Green Gator," a story about jealousy in Easy's life and among his clients. The last two stories in the volume, though, are the most important. Despite Etta's claims that she buried Mouse in the desert, he nevertheless reappears—alive and well—and just knocks on Easy's door at the beginning of "Silver Linings," a story that reflects Easy's past in Texas as Easy helps exonerate Momma Jo's son Dom, when he has been falsely accused of robbing an armored car. Similarly, in the final story, "Amber Gate," Easy tries to prove that his client, Musa Tanous, did not kill his young girlfriend, Jackie. Easy realizes that Harold, a misogynistic and homicidal hobo, killed Jackie because he hated her for dating a white man. As payment for his assistance, Tanous leases Easy an office at a drastically reduced rate, and near the end of the tale, Easy reports, "I put up a sign on my amber door. It reads: Easy Rawlins / Research and Delivery" (278).

Little Scarlet (no subtitle, 2004; dedicated to the late dancer Gregory Hines) begins just as the 1965 Watts riots are ending. Easy has finally ventured out of his house to survey the damage to his office and the surrounding neighborhoods. At his office, he encounters Melvin Suggs, an LAPD detective who wants Easy's help solving the murder of a young black woman named Nola Payne. The police believe Nola was killed by a white man during the final days of the riots, and Suggs takes Easy to the Miller Neurological Sanatorium, where Easy meets Deputy Commissioner Gerald Jordan, who is sanctioning the investigation. There Easy also interviews Nola's aunt, Geneva Landry, who has been driven insane by the overwhelming violence of the riots and her niece's grizzly death. Geneva tells Easy and the police that Nola took in a white man who had been attacked while driving his car through the neighborhood during the riots and that the white man then killed Nola. The police explain that they need Easy to investigate the murder quickly and quietly because they are afraid that the riots will start anew if the public hears that a white man murdered a black woman in Watts.

By asking questions around the neighborhood and with the particular help of an attractive young woman named Juanda, Easy quickly determines that the white man Nola saved was Peter Rhone, a supervisor at the company where Nola worked as a switchboard operator. When Easy confronts Rhone and tells him about Nola's death, the despondent Rhone explains that he was in love with Nola. Not convinced that Rhone is Nola's killer, Easy continues investigating until he realizes that Nola was killed by Harold, the same deranged vagabond who killed Jackie in the *Six Easy Pieces* story "Amber Gate."

Easy then spends the last half of the novel trying to find Harold and bring him to justice—or kill him. The search leads Easy to Harold's childhood home and the white woman, Jocelyn Ostenberg, who raised him after his mother, the woman's housekeeper, left. Easy comes to realize, though, that the white woman is not Harold's guardian, but his mother, who is passing for white and therefore could not acknowledge the dark-skinned Harold as her own. This maternal betrayal now fuels Harold's homicidal rage against black women who love white men. The streetwise Harold continues to elude Easy and Suggs. Suggs becomes an unexpected ally of the LAPD and links Harold to over twenty other solved and unsolved murders. Jordan pressures Easy and Suggs to turn over Rhone so the LAPD can close the case. Easy threatens to expose Jocelyn unless she helps him find Harold; she reluctantly agrees, but Harold kills her after also trying to kill Easy. Wounded by Jocelyn before he kills her, Harold seeks refuge with another former caretaker, Honey May, who poisons him to stop his killing spree. Easy and Mouse dump the body, along with the gun incriminating him in Nola's death, in a vacant lot, where the police later discover him. Despite his frustration with Easy's irreverence, Jordan rewards Easy with a private investigator's license.

In *Cinnamon Kiss* (no subtitle, 2005; dedicated to the late Ossie Davis, "our shining king"), set in 1966, Easy takes on his first case as a legitimate private investigator. The story opens with Easy and Mouse plotting an armored-car heist that will get them part of the money that Easy needs to pay a Swiss hospital to cure Feather's rare blood infection. In anticipation of these criminal activities and despite his rich principal's offers to help, Easy even takes an indefinite leave of absence from his beloved post at Sojourner Truth Junior High School. Before Easy is forced into a life of crime, however, Saul Lynx comes through with a job working for a San Francisco private investigator named Robert E. Lee. Lee and his beautiful assistant, Maya Adament, hire Easy to find Axel Bowers, a Berkeley lawyer, and his lover/assistant Philomena "Cinnamon" Cargill, who have allegedly absconded with papers that are important to Lee's client. Lee is outsourcing part of the investigation to Easy because of Cinnamon's Watts connections.

Rather than return immediately to Los Angeles, though, Easy decides to stay in San Francisco and check out Bowers's house. There, in a backyard shrine, he finds Bowers's mangled and decomposing body under a trunk of old pornography and Nazi paraphernalia. Exploring many of the same neighborhoods that were the backdrop for Mosley's enigmatic science-fiction novel *Blue Light,* Easy encounters hippie subculture for the first time as he visits Axel's associates—including his business partner, Claudia Obek, and his father's business partner (and Lee's client), Leonard Haffernon. In Cinnamon's apartment, which she clearly left hastily, he finds a postcard from Lena McAllister, a woman he knows in Los Angeles.

Easy returns home to continue the search and to send Feather and Bonnie to Switzerland to start Feather's treatments, which Bonnie reveals are being sponsored by her former paramour, the African prince Jogyue Cham. Easy finds Cinnamon, and she explains that the papers Haffernon wants are Swiss bonds accompanied by a note detailing Axel's family's dealing with the Nazis. When an assassin starts threatening Easy and Cinnamon, though, Easy realizes that there is more to the investigation than Lee has revealed, so Easy and Saul reach out to Christmas Black, a former soldier, who along with Mouse helps the detectives make a plan to expose Lee. Cicero shoots Lee, though, and Easy connects the attempt to Maya Adament, who hired the killer to help her get the bonds and her revenge on Lee for being a tyrannical employer. With Cicero still at large, Cinnamon helps Easy connect the bonds back to Claudia Aubeck's family. Easy returns to San Francisco to confront her, but he finds that she has been shot by Cicero, who soon dies from the poison Claudia put in his tea before he shot her.

In *Blonde Faith: An Easy Rawlins Novel* (2007; "In memory of August Wilson"), set in 1967, Easy comes home from a case to find that Christmas Black has left his daughter, Easter Dawn, for Easy to care for. Easy calls around to his friends, trying to find Christmas. When he calls Mouse's house, though, Etta tells Easy that Mouse is wanted for killing a friend, Pericles (Perry) Tarr, and she asks Easy for help because she is worried the cops will kill Mouse. Now looking for both Mouse and Christmas, Easy searches Christmas's old apartment, where he meets a soldier who introduces himself as Captain Clarence Miles, and Miles asks Easy if he will help the United States government find Christmas. Easy is suspicious of Miles, especially when Miles pays him in cash, but Easy still takes the job. Easy also tracks down another recent address for Christmas, and upon arriving there, he finds two soldiers' bodies but no Christmas. Evidence from the house, though, leads Easy to the beautiful blonde Faith Morel, a humanitarian worker whom Christmas met in Vietnam after he killed everyone in Easter Dawn's village. Faith confirms that Miles is actually Sammy Sansoam, a military policeman turned mercenary, and that he is very dangerous. The next day, Sansoam murders Faith.

Meanwhile, Easy continues to look for Mouse. Perry's "widow," Meredith, is convinced that her husband is dead and that Mouse killed him when Perry would not pay back a loan; Easy, however, is unconvinced, especially when he learns through his neighborhood contacts that Perry was Mouse's business partner and that he was planning to leave his wife. Easy decides to track down Perry's mistress, Pretty Smart, who leads him to Perry. When Easy threatens to tie Perry up and bring him back to his family, he gives Easy an address for Mouse.

At this address, Christmas answers the door. Not surprised that the two killers have joined forces, Easy updates his friends on his investigation and tells them about Faith's murder. The group then plans to avenge Faith. Easy calls in a fake tip to the police, telling them where Mouse will be, and then sets up a meet with the fake soldiers for the same location. Both parties in place, Easy fires a shot at the police, setting off a gun battle that destroys the house with the soldiers in it. Easy, depressed and disillusioned over the recent events and losing Bonnie, turns to drinking, drives his car off a cliff, and describes his own death.

Little Green: An Easy Rawlins Mystery (2013; no dedication), set a few weeks after *Blonde Faith*, opens with Easy recounting the feelings and visions he had as he was dying after his accident. He awakens, though, to Mouse's girlfriend, Lynne, keeping watch over him. She explains that Easy had been presumed dead after he drove over the cliff, but Jo told Mouse that he needed to go looking for Easy near the crash site. Mouse found him and carried his nearly lifeless body back to Jo, who nursed him for a while before sending him, still unconscious, back to his family. Easy is not awake for long, though, before Mouse asks him to help find a missing young man, Evander "Little Green" Noon. Against his nurse's orders and his family's wishes—and with a boost from "Gator's Blood," one of Jo's voodoo elixirs—Easy takes the case. Mouse has a connection to the Noon family and to Evander especially, but he's unwilling to reveal details. Evander's mother, Timbale, is similarly elusive but makes it clear that she hates Mouse and wants him dead.

The last time Timbale heard from Evander, he was headed to a discotheque with a white hippie. So, Easy heads to Sunset Boulevard to ask questions, and he finds out that Evander had a bad LSD trip with a woman named Ruby, and he was crazy for days. Easy eventually rescues Evander from a Santa Monica commune, and although he at first cannot recall how he got there or why the white men there were beating him, he eventually remembers that he had been involved in a drug deal gone bad and had fled with the criminals' blood-soaked money. Easy hides Evander, and they sort out whose money it is and who is still hunting down Evander for it.

Jackson Blue's boss, Jean-Paul Villard, agrees to hide the bloody money, but Jean-Paul and Jackson also ask Easy for help stopping a blackmailer who claims to have Jackson's fingerprints on a gun that can be tied to an unsolved murder. The blackmailers threaten to give the gun to the police unless Jackson helps embezzle millions of dollars of Jean-Paul's money. Easy, Jackson, and Mouse find the man, Charles Rumor, who likely got the fingerprints off one of Jackson's other guns. He gives up the gun and the men who hired him. Easy then arranges a setup that will expose the blackmailers and save Jean-Paul's investments.

Meanwhile, Easy continues to help Evander and thwart the men who are after him. Easy learns that one is already dead, finds another tortured and murdered, and works his police contacts to get the last one arrested. Before he can do this, though, the white man, Keith Handel, comes after Easy, who kills him in self-defense. Knowing that killing a white man would certainly lead to his own death—for real this time—Easy along with Mouse disposes of the body in Jo's "backyard vat." Easy also prevents Evander from trying to kill Mouse after Timbale reveals that Mouse had killed Evander's father, Frank Green from *Devil in a Blue Dress*.

In *Rose Gold: An Easy Rawlins Mystery* (2014; dedicated to Amiri Baraka), Easy is moving into a new house just a few months after the events of *Little Green*. While he and his friends unpack the moving truck, a group of police— led by Robert Frisk, special assistant to the chief of police—approach Easy about investigating the disappearance (and potential kidnapping) of white heiress Rosemary Goldsmith (Rose Gold), a student at the University of California, Santa Barbara. Rosemary was last seen with her black boyfriend, boxer Bob Mantle, also known as Uhuru Nolice, who is wanted in connection with a series of shootings, including one that killed three police officers. The police and Rosemary's father, weapons manufacturer Foster Goldsmith, worry that her disappearance might be politically motivated.

Easy starts to go undercover at the gym where Mantle practices and teaches, but someone tries to kill him; this attempt on his life, combined with the FBI and the State Department demanding that Easy back off the case, leads him to realize that the case may be more dangerous than he initially suspected. So he enlists the help of disgraced LAPD detective Suggs as well as some of his former hippie contacts. Through these resources, Easy eventually tracks down Bob, who claims that he did not kill anyone and that he does not know where Rosemary is. Easy believes him.

The search for Rosemary becomes more urgent, however, when the family finally receives ransom demands, along with one of Rosemary's fingers. Easy and his associates eventually track Rosemary to a revolutionary named Most Grand. They determine that the pair planned the ransom hoax, but the relationship has deteriorated. So they arrange a setup under the guise of giving the captor the ransom. At the staged handoff, there is a shootout; the captors are killed, Rosemary is liberated, and Bob is exonerated. At the end of the novel, Easy tells Mouse about his plans to set up a staffed detective agency in downtown Los Angeles.

Where Easy Is Going

In a span of two decades, of course, everyone changes—and not just in their views on love, friendship, and race. The changes outlined here are just a representative sampling of the myriad ways that Easy's character evolves over his more than a dozen texts.

Relationships

Among Easy's most notable and earliest changes is in his understanding and treatment of women. Generally, the women in the novels do not take on domestic roles; Easy and his children run their home. Even when Easy does live with a woman, it is in *his* house, and her domestic responsibilities are self-assumed and largely unnoticed by Easy. In *A Red Death,* Easy does reflect on his mother baking sweet-potato pies for the church even when she was ill, but this reflection more likely arises from Easy's love of food and cooking than his desire to relegate her to a domestic role; otherwise, his memories of her focus on her untimely death at twenty-five—a formative loss that leaves him to face the world alone (88).[2] Even as he dies at the end of *Blonde Faith,* he looks for her in his mind's eye, but she remains absent (308).

Although Easy does not relegate women to domestic roles, he does, at least initially, sexualize them. In his first two novels, Easy sleeps with multiple women but has no lasting emotional connections. By the third novel, *White Butterfly,* though, Easy has a wife, Regina, and a daughter. Regina, however, worries about Easy's emotional distance and her place in his life. Their relationship deteriorates irrevocably after a sexual encounter that the two of them interpret very differently. Regina tells Easy, "What you did to me. I didn't want non 'a you. But you made me. You raped me" (33).[3] Easy responds: "'Rape.' I laughed. 'Man cain't rape his own wife'" (39).

Despite this initial dismissal, Easy eventually begins to realize, "It seemed like I was on the warpath against women and that all the men I knew, and those I didn't know, were too" (92). When Easy and Regina come back to the topic of the sexual encounter later in the novel, Easy is already trying to embrace a new perspective. He reflects: "I didn't know what to say then. I thought about what she called rape. I didn't think that it was like some of these men do to women, how they grab them off the street and brutalize them. But I knew that if she was unwilling then I made her against that will. I was wrong but I didn't have the heart to admit it" (136).

Critic Roger A. Berger suggests "there is a sense that Mosley criticizes Rawlins's relentless heterosexuality, for at the end of each novel, we find a chastened and psychologically shattered Rawlins almost completely alone."[4] Easy's sexual prowess does not underscores his masculinity and strength; rather, it detracts from them.

The Easy Rawlins of *Little Scarlet,* though, looks like a feminist in contrast to his former self. After hearing Geneva Landry's story of violence and sacrifice, he realizes that the same violence could "happen to any black woman. She had to take mountains of abuse while protecting her blood. She could never speak about the atrocities done to her while at the same time she dressed the wounds of her loved ones" (121). In this novel, Easy is plagued by nightmares of murdered women hanging in a meat locker because he is not able to stop their killer. He still speaks admirably of women and their passion, despite their vulnerability. When Mouse mistreats his girlfriend, Easy reminds him, "Black women, Ray. You know how they are. Tough as you ever wanna be. Go up against a whole gang to protect her man. Ready to walk away if you do her wrong the next day" (229).

Easy's relationship with his other mother figure, Mama/Mamma Jo (the novels alternate spellings), follows a similar pattern. His initial relationship with her, as detailed in *Gone Fishin',* is sexual. However, in a repetition and reversal of his sexual dominance over Regina, sex with Jo scares Easy. He remembers, "I didn't want to do it but Momma Jo was strong; she clenched her arms and legs around me so powerfully that my 'No' was crushed down to 'Yes.' She whispered in my ear what she wanted and I lost my mind for a while; lost it to her desire" (62).[5] He thus fears her at first, but he eventually embraces this power over him and sees Jo as an Earth Mother. He comes to her when he needs physical healing, and it is she who "feels" that he is still alive after the crash and sends Mouse to find him. A victim of sexual violence herself—her late husband kidnapped and raped her when she was a young girl—Jo represents the strength of black womanhood, and her more frequent appearance in the later novels reinforces Easy's move away from relying on a purely sexual view of womanhood.

Easy's most important female relationship, though, is with the love of his life, Bonnie Shay. Bonnie affects not only the content of the novels but also their titles. Most of the Easy Rawlins novels/mysteries take their titles from women's names or nicknames. Each novel in the series that does not follow this pattern—by using a man's name or a dog's—focuses, at least in part, on key *positive* developments in Easy's relationship with Bonnie. He meets and falls in love with her in *A Little Yellow Dog,* they are living together happily in *Bad Boy Brawley Brown,* and they rekindle their romance in *Little Green.*

After Regina leaves, Easy has no significant long-term relationships until he meets Bonnie. Right away, he feels a profound connection to her. He notes,

"Her face was full of feelings and memories that I thought I might know" (92).[6] He also feels able—and almost compelled—to share the most intimate, otherwise hidden, details of his life with her, even if it makes him vulnerable. Near the end of *A Little Yellow Dog*, for example, he tells her, "I'm a simple man, Miss Shay. I'm a head custodian for the Board of Education and I own a few apartment buildin's here and there"; then, he realizes, "that was the first time in my life that I told somebody about what I had just in conversation. Where I came from you kept everything a secret—survival depended on keeping people around you in the dark" (255). Her effect on him is so profound he feels as if she has altered his entire universe: "I was an astronaut who had completed his orbit of the earth and now I was pulled by some new gravity into a cold clean darkness" (375).

As Easy's love for her deepens, Bonnie inspires him and reminds him of his potential for greatness, but she also opens him up to the potential for profound pain. When he struggles with the weight of the case in *Little Scarlet*, Bonnie tells Easy, "Be our hero" (94),[7] and in *Blonde Faith*, she tells him, "'You're not some men[. . . .] You're Easy Rawlins" (305).[8] She encourages him, never questions his work, and loves his children as her own.

When this love forces her to betray Easy, though, the pain sends him into a self-destructive downward spiral that leads to his near-fatal crash. Bonnie reunites with her former lover Jogyue Cham to help get Feather the medical treatment she needs in *Cinnamon Kiss*, but Easy's pride prevents him from seeing the personal sacrifice in her betrayal, and he sends her away. In *Blonde Faith*, then, he mourns his loss, seeking temporary solace in the bedrooms of multiple women until he has an epiphany: "I got to see what I had become," and he decides: "I could not live without Bonnie[. . . .] Either I was going to be back with her or, one way or another, I was going to die" (146). This epiphany marks the first time that Easy sees his life as quintessentially intertwined with another's. He loves Mouse and his children, but neither Mouse's "death" nor Feather's life-threatening illness has this profound effect on him. And when Bonnie tells him that she is engaged to Jogyue and will not come back to Easy, his life does nearly end.

Bonnie's trust in and love for Easy also show that he has changed significantly since his relationship with Regina. After she hears that Easy is presumed dead, but before she learns he is still alive, she breaks off her engagement to Jogyue. She explains to Easy in *Little Green* that Jogyue "didn't understand her choice"; "He is royalty and rich, a part of a world that no black American or Caribbean could even really understand or imagine. But I told him your were my man, dead or alive" (146).[9] She loves Easy because he helps her understand herself and her racial identity. Their relationship does not just fulfill Easy's physical needs, it fulfills both Easy's and Bonnie's emotional and social needs. Their healing—chronicled in *Little Green,* and, less prominently, in *Rose Gold*—is slow, but it is a key element in Easy's healing from his near-death experience.

This healing is only possible, though, because of Mouse, Easy's best friend and the most important recurring character in the series. This relationship, though—like Easy's relationship with Bonnie and the other women in the novel—is far from straightforward and changes considerably over the course of the series, reflecting on how the friendship between the two men shapes and is shaped by Easy's strengths and flaws. In the early mystery novels and in the re-flective *Gone Fishin',* Mouse appears as a ruthless killer that Easy barely trusts but needs as backup for potentially violent situations. Mouse's violence, according to critic Marilyn C. Wesley, "[suggests] the restriction of black power to defensive reaction in a white world of superior control." [10]

In *Devil in A Blue Dress,* Mouse tells Easy, "you gotta have somebody at yo' back man. That's just a lie them white men give 'bout making it on they own. They always got they backs covered" (153).[11] Mouse is essentially just a weapon or a bodyguard for Easy. The emotional connection is not developed, and Easy even tells his business associate Mofass, "I ain't got no friends, man. All I got is Jack Blue, who'd give me up fo' a bottle 'a wine, and Mouse; you know him" (245). Easy then asks Mofass to be his friend. His reply—"Sure[. . . .] You my best customer, Mr. Rawlins," suggests that such a friendship is impossible be-cause the sick man is incapable of seeing beyond their economic relationship (245).

Gone Fishin', which Mosley wrote before *Devil* but did not publish until after *A Little Yellow Dog,* provides some explanation for Easy's distrust of Mouse. At the beginning of this coming-of-age story, Easy calls Mouse "my only real friend, and even though he was crazy and wild I knew he cared for me—in his way. He made me mad sometimes but that is what good friends and family do" (16–17). As the violent events of that novel unfold, however, Easy begins to feel responsible for his hot-headed friend. He explains, "I had driven Mouse out there and anything he did was a reflection on me" (195). And after he confronts Mouse about killing Reese, Easy does not want to take his share of Reese's money, but Mouse tells him, "You the on'y one who know why I come down here an' you the on'y one who know what happened. If you don't take that money then I know you against me" (218). Feeling bullied and trapped, Easy decides he needs to leave Houston and redefine himself outside of the reach of Mouse's influence: "I needed a place where life was a little easier and where nobody knew me. I knew that if I could be alone I could make it" (237).

By the time of *White Butterfly,* though, Easy is able to see some value in his relationship with Mouse as well as value in the man himself. When Mouse is arrested, Easy says, "It made me sick at heart to see Raymond like that. He was the only black man I'd ever known who had never been chained, in his mind, by the white man. Mouse was brash and wild and free. He might have been insane, but any Negro who dared to believe in his own freedom in American had to be mad" (145). Although there is still a distance between them because Mouse and Mofass "weren't friends that you could kick back and jaw with" (179), Easy also comes to realize that "Mouse had a way of bringing out the love in people. It was because there was no shame in him. For the desperate souls in us all, Mouse was a savior. He brought out the dreams you had as a baby. He made you believe in magic again. He was the kind of devil you'd sell your soul to and never regret the deal" (222).

Despite this new understanding of Mouse's innate "magic," Easy still feels alone—until, that is, he is able to realize that Raymond's roughness is a necessary complement to the life Easy has chosen. He pines in *Black Betty*, "I wished that I had some kind of brother at arms to rely on. All I ever had was Mouse, and standing side by side with him was like pressing up against a porcupine" (227).[12] But in the next novel, *A Little Yellow Dog*, Easy realizes that "a porcupine" might be just what he needs after all. He reflects, "In the hard life of the streets you needed somebody like Mouse at your back. I didn't have a mother or father, or close family or church. All I had was my friends. And among them Mouse packed the largest caliber and hardest of rock-hard wills" (63). So, when Mouse is shot at the end of this novel, Easy feels profound and revealing loss. To illustrate the depth of this loss, the text parallels Mouse's "assassination" with John F. Kennedy's. Easy remembers, "I turned on the radio and the TV. Both of them droned on about the assassination. I didn't understand a word of it but the sad sound of grief resonated in my heart. My best friend was wounded somewhere, maybe he was dead. It was my fault and I couldn't even go to him and tell him that I was sorry" (361).

As he continues to grieve for Mouse, Easy's love for his lost friend intensifies, as does Mouse's influence—even in absence—over his life. In *Bad Boy Brawley Brown*, Easy memorializes, "Raymond Alexander was the most perfect human being a black man could imagine. He was a lover and killer and one of the best storytellers you ever heard" (237).[13] In this novel, Mouse comes to Easy in visions and tells him how to solve the case, thereby reinforcing Easy's connection to his lifelong friend—a connection that he did not realize the depths of until Mouse was gone. Easy realizes, in particular, "My respect for Raymond was intense because he never worried about or second-guessed the world around him. He might have gotten tired now and then, but he never gave up. When I thought about that, I knew I had to go search out his grave" (305). Mouse helped Easy take the world less personally and focus instead on his own actions and motivations, so Easy needs to know Mouse's fate in order to understand his own.

When Ray walks, nonchalantly, back into Easy's life in *Six Easy Pieces,* the two are close friends for the rest of the series, and their friendship focuses on mutual accountability. In *Cinnamon Kiss,* for example, Easy comes to understand, "One of my special duties was to keep Raymond Alexander from falling into a deep humor. Because whenever he lost his interest in having a good time someone, somewhere, was likely to die" (188).[14] Rather than question Mouse's violence, Easy comes to see the necessity of that violence. Mouse, Easy says, "was the kind of man who stood there beside you through blood and fire, death and torture. No one would ever choose to live in a world where they'd need a friend like Mouse, but you don't choose the world you live in or the skin you inhabit" (75). And by *Little Green,* Easy clearly needs Mouse. Mouse keeps him from killing Jackson Blue's blackmailer when he is blinded by the rage Jo's Gator Juice inspires, and Mouse helps him hide the body of the white man Easy kills at the end of the novel. But more significantly, Easy sees the truth in Jo's touching observation about Easy's "resurrection": "You were down in the pit and it was Raymond's love that dragged you out. You two is just like chirren on a seesaw. One 'a you is up and the other one down. That's how it goes" (68).

Race

As Easy navigates these personal relationships, he also makes his way through an ever-challenging racial landscape. At the beginning of *Devil in a Blue Dress,* Easy states clearly, "I felt I was just as good as any white man" (9). However, he is disillusioned by his inability to stand up to white hatred, by his memories of the racism he experienced as a soldier in World War II, and by the seemingly unending police brutality he and his associates endure.

When Easy and Mouse discover, at the end of the novel, that Daphne Monet has been passing for white, Mouse chastises, "That's just like you, Easy. You learn stuff and you be thinkin' like white men be thinkin'. You be thinkin' that what's right fo' them is right fo' you. She look like she white and you think like you white. But brother you don't know that you both poor niggers. And a nigger ain't never gonna be happy 'less he accept what he is" (205). According to critic Nicole King, "Mouse's comments effectively link the novel's passing discourse with its discourse of racial uplift. His negative evaluations of both Daphne/Ruby and Easy incisively expose how each has swallowed the myth of the American Dream and recklessly believes it applies to him or her."[15] In short, the impact of racism, at this point in his life, puts a strain in Easy's own racial identity. Even as he reads Plato in *White Butterfly,* "I wondered at how it would be to be a white man; a man who felt that he belonged" (8).

Easy is simultaneously very distrustful of white Americans. When Chaim Wenzler put his hand on Easy in *A Red Death*, Easy says, "I never knew a white man who thought that we were *really* the same. When he touched my arm he might as well have stuck his hand in my chest and grabbed my heart" (121). Later in the novel, he elaborates, "I trusted a Negro, I don't know why. I'd been beaten, robbed, shot at, and generally mistreated by more colored brothers than I'd ever been by whites, but I trusted a black man before I'd even think about a white one. That's just the way things were for me" (143). Easy is constantly on the lookout for white men, especially white cops, who want to harm him, or even kill him.

By *Black Betty*, though, Easy begins to feel hope for some positive change for race relations in America. After waking up from a nightmare about one of Mouse's murders, he "tried to think of better things. About our new young Irish president and Martin Luther King; about how the world was changing and a black man in America had the chance to be a man for the first time in hundreds of years" (3). Then, when he stands up to a racist clerk later in the novel, he thinks: "I wasn't marching or singing songs about freedom. I didn't pay dues in the Southern Christian Leadership Conference or the NAACP. I didn't have any kind of god on my side. But even though the cameras weren't on me and JFK had never heard my name, I had to make my little stand for what's right. It was a little piece of history that happened right there in that room and that went unrecorded" (195).

He feels connected to a larger community and to a national movement, even though he is not officially affiliated with these efforts. This connection suggests that Easy sees the value of individual change to the collective whole. A movement can start with just one man.

Easy also finds some freedom and hope in reading—especially reading literature. *Gone Fishin'*'s chronological disruption in the series is not only valuable for deciphering the roots of Easy's relationship with Mouse, but also for understanding the racialized roots of Easy's literacy. Easy's father, the labor organizer, had always pushed Easy to learn how to read, but it is not until he meets Jo's son Dom and his white teacher-benefactor Miss Dixon that he begins to see the value of literacy for self and community uplift. Dom recounts that Dixon taught him to read so that he could better understand the Bible: "She say that to know the word you gotta make the Bible yo' own. You gotta know the stories just like they happened t' friends 'a yours" (84).

This observation, in concert with his memories of his father, leads Easy to the epiphany that he needs to learn to read. He explains, "I thought that if I could read I wouldn't have to hang around people like Mouse to tell me stories, I could just read stories myself. And if I didn't like the stories I read then I could just change them the way that Dom did with the Bible" (133). Easy comes to see reading as a source of power, not only because of the knowledge that it brings, but also because of the control that it offers readers over their own destiny. Reading and interpreting literature and history give Easy a framework for understanding himself and his cultural contexts. In the remaining novels, Easy describes reading works such as Claude McKay's *Banjo*, Ralph Ellison's *Invisible Man*, and Chester Himes's *Cotton Comes to Harlem*.

Easy does not, however, believe everything he reads. In particular, he is unwilling to fully embrace the more militant sentiments espoused by the Urban Revolutionary Party in *Bad Boy Brawley Brown*. Based on the histories—white and black—that he has read, Easy sees nothing new in their "blurred" pamphlet (29), and although he applauds their idealistic attempt to "create freedom out of the sow's ear called America" (44), he also notes—nodding to his numerous run-ins with the racist LAPD—"There was not an Emancipation Proclamation posted on the jailhouse bulletin board. No Bill of Rights, either" (69). Similarly, when party leader Henry Strong asks Easy if he is "a Race man," Easy replies, "I can run if I have to"; when Strong tries to clarify, Easy comes back, "I know what you meant. You one 'a them better-than-thou kind Negros tryin' to explain everything by your own book. But I'm just an everyday black man, doin' the best I can in a world where the white man's de facto king." (130). Easy has little tolerance for abstract political philosophies; he is focused on the tangible day-to-day life of African Americans in Los Angeles.

And this life is changed forever by the series's most significant historical event: the 1965 Watts riots. Easy, like Mosley's own father, resists the urge to join the rioters because he fears for his family's safety. When Feather, in *Little Scarlet*, asks Easy why he was crying while watching TV during the riots, he explains—in prose that closely parallels Mosley's father's story, as retold in *Working on the Chain Gang*:

> I was watching images of the rioters on the late news with the volume turned off, witnessing those poor souls out in the street fighting against an enemy that I recognized just as well as they. I had read the newspapers and heard the commentaries from the white newscasters. But my point of view was never aired. I didn't want the violence but I was tired of policemen stopping me just for walking down the street. I hated the destruction of property and life, but what good was law and order if it meant I was supposed to ignore the fact that our children were treated like little hoodlums or whores? My patience was as thin as a Liberty dime, but still I stayed in my house to protect my makeshift family. That's what brought me to tears. But how could I say all that to a ten-year-old girl? (43)

After the riots, though, the rage Easy felt when he watched the fighting from afar—combined with the rage born from years to oppression—fuels him. He feels "it was as though there was a strong wind at my back. I had resisted it all through the riots: the angry voice in my heart that urged me to go out and fight after all of the hangings I had seen, after all of the times I had been called nigger and all of the doors that had been slammed in my face" (18). Nearly all of *Little Scarlet* addresses the riots—their root causes and their effects, both short-term and long-term.

In the texts that follow, Easy continues to comment on the riots' personal, cultural, and financial effects. In particular, the riots lead Easy, albeit sometimes indirectly, to have positive interactions, even friendships with, white men—a move that the Easy of *Devil in Blue Dress* likely would have deemed preposterous. While his interactions with white women remain primarily sexual, he finds solidarity and sometimes kinship in his relationships with white men. His search for the murderous Harold in *Little Scarlet,* for example, leads to his friendship with LAPD detective Melvin Suggs, who becomes such an ally in later stories that Easy calls him "a good cop" in *Blonde Faith* (209). In this same novel, Easy observes, "Maybe 15 or 20 percent of the white people I met tried to get a leg up over me. It wasn't the majority of folks—but it sure felt like it" (79). He is even able to have a frank discussion of white privilege with a white restaurant owner after the restaurant's racist hostess is rude to Easy (90), and he feels a kinship with the hippies who remind him of black parties in the South because "you could feel the hope coming off of them in waves" (83). These subtle yet significant changes show that Easy's world is changing and that Easy is changing with it. While he still encounters significant racism, he also encounters kindness—even though he is still, most often, surprised by that kindness. He still lives in "a they-and-us world," but sometimes the "they" and "us" manage to cooperate in a way that meets Easy's needs.

This post-riot Los Angeles theme takes on even more significance, though, in *Little Green* because Easy parallels his own death and resurrection to the black community's during the riots and their aftermath. As he drives through Watts, he observes, "There were still lots of boarded-up, burned-out buildings that indicated the businesses that had yet to return to the 'hood after the devastating riots. My community has suffered decimation *as I had*. It was trying to come back, but there was no promise that it would rise again either" (128, emphasis added). Easy, again, sees some hope and potential white solidarity when a group of white mechanics and the white garage owner stand up to two racist white cops who harass Easy and one of their coworkers. He reports, "I had the definite feeling that while I was dead, the world had changed somewhat" (48).

Again, this change is not compelling or widespread enough to prevent Easy from encountering racism. The changes in Easy himself, though, mitigate its effects. As he confronts the racist white clerk at Jackson Blue's office, he describes his emotions:

> The feeling arising in my breast was at once familiar and alien[. . . .] Along with anxiety and fear my people had inherited spite and rage for the centuries of oppression that we were reminded of almost every day of our lives. To experience the malice of generations in a moment is a taste so bitter that it could make an otherwise healthy man retch.
>
> I saw this emotion in my imagined reflection in the young man's blue eyes, but I didn't feel a thing. I had died and there was nothing that anyone could do to match the experience of my semiresurrection. (166)

This rejection of double-consciousness is complete and liberating. Easy sees himself, hated, through the white clerk's eyes, "the eyes of the other,"[16] but he can ignore that representation because of this new, stronger, more history-focused identity born of his powerful experience. After his "death" and "semi-resurrection," Easy—like Watts—emerges with a clear sense of identity shaped less by white hatred and more by shared history.

Genre

How much and in what ways Easy evolves over the course of his narrative also has implications for where his stories fit in the mystery genre. Most critics writing about Easy call him some variation on "hard-boiled" or "noir," channeling the foundational concepts in mystery fiction. But Easy—especially since he is not a professional detective at the start of the series—does not perfectly fit any of the traditional mystery models.

In his pioneering 1948 essay, "The Guilty Vicarage: Notes on the Detective Story, by an Addict," W. H. Auden explains that pure detective stories follow a "basic formula," in which "a murder occurs; many are suspects; all but one suspect, who is the murderer, are eliminated; the murderer is arrested or dies" (406). This formula could apply to many of the Easy Rawlins texts. There is always a murder (or many), Easy must—through a series of suspenseful events—logically eliminate suspects or track them down, and the murderers are usually killed or captured.

However, Auden's description of the detective himself is much less applicable. Auden writes, "the detective must be either the official representative of the ethical or the exceptional individual who is himself in a state of grace."[17] Easy is neither. He earns his private investigator's license by working for the nefarious Assistant Police Commissioner Gerald Jordan in *Little Scarlet*, but he does not regard Jordan as "ethical." And while Easy is certainly a man of strong principles, it is not ethics, but rather self or community preservation—sometimes even money—that motivates his work. In *A Red Death,* for example, the IRS and FBI, threatening Easy with tax-evasion charges, pressure him to investigate Chaim Wenzler. They want Easy not because he is ethical, but because he is black and "the FBI couldn't really mount an investigation in the ghetto" (95). In *White Butterfly,* he reiterates, "Every once in a while the law sent over one of their few black representatives to ask me to go into places where they could never go. I was worth a precinct full of detectives when the cops needed the word in the ghetto" (2).

Auden also stipulates that "the detective must be the total stranger who cannot possibly be involved in the crime."[18] When Easy is not working for the cops to avoid trouble, however, he is working for favors from friends, and he is consistently arrested for his potential connections to the crimes he is investigating. In *A Little Yellow Dog* in particular, Easy is the police's prime suspect in the novel's first murder as well as a series of robberies the police believe led to that murder. Easy must also step in when the law cannot or will not, or when the law itself is an aggressor in the case. He explains, again in *White Butterfly,* "In my time I had done work for the numbers runners, churchgoers, businessmen, and even the police. Somewhere along the line I had slipped into the role of a confidential agent who represented people when the law broke down" (9–10).

Easy fits better into Raymond Chandler's definition of the detective from "The Simple Art of Murder" (1950): "He is the hero, he is everything. He must be a complete man and a common man and yet an unusual man."[19] Easy understands that, as a "common" black man, with intimate knowledge of his community, he is uniquely positioned to investigate events within or affecting that community. However, Chandler also writes that the detective must be "a good enough man for any world."[20] This is a problem for Easy because the racist world in which he operates will never think him "good enough."

New York Times critic Richard Bernstein suggests that in both the Easy Rawlins and Fearless Jones novels Mosley has pioneered "a kind of double noir: the stylistic noir of the detective story and the racial noir of Los Angeles in the mid-1950's."[21] In her article "Race in American Crime Fiction," Maureen Reddy explores this idea in detail. She argues that "black-authored hard-boiled detectives," such as Easy Rawlins, challenge "the centrality of whiteness to the genre" and "modify the conventional solitariness of the detective by embedding the black detective in a community"; these detectives also serve as "correctives to dominant, racist stereotypes of black men as violent, dangerous, over-sexed predators unfit for civilized society, absent from their children, lazy, unwilling to work hard at anything."[22] Easy for example understands, even by *Black Betty,* that "the world wasn't going to let me be an upright businessman" (12), so, as he tries to explain to the cops in A *Little Yellow Dog,* "What I do I do because it's a part of me. I studied in the streets and back alleys. What I know most cops would give their eyeteeth to understand. So don't worry about how I got here or how to explain what I do. Just listen to me and you might learn somethin'" (213).

In essence, the double noir or black hard-boiled is a genre-upending genre. Easy fits in this genre because he does not fit anywhere else. He is, as he says twice in *Little Green,* "a rare breed" (40, 82). Black detectives operate in a white-dominated world that either will not allow them access to "typical" experience or makes that experience devoid of meaning because it so inapplicable to black identity and black community. Easy happily reflects at the end of his "semiresurrection," "I was a man again, on the job again, back in the world where nothing ever turned out right but it kept right on turning anyway" (265).

CHAPTER THREE

Becoming Fearless
Symbiotic Identity in *Fearless Jones*

Nathaniel Hawthorne's 1850 short story "Ethan Brand: A Chapter from an Abortive Romance" explores the "Unpardonable Sin," which is essentially a separation of the intellectual and the human—or, more simply—of mind and heart. In the story, protagonist Ethan Brand reveals, "It is a sin that grew within my own breast[. . . .] The sin of an intellect that triumphed over the sense of brotherhood with man and reverence for God, and sacrificed everything to its own mighty claims!" [1] At the opening of *Fearless Jones* (2001), narrator Paris Minton has separated himself from his best friend, Fearless, the eponymous hero of the novel, and thus unwittingly banished himself to a lonely and cowardly life.

The novel portrays Paris and Fearless's friendship as symbiotic: Fearless humanizes the potentially misanthropic Paris, and Paris tames Fearless's murderous rage. Paris benefits more from this arrangement, though, because, as the novel progresses, Paris, plagued by fear, finds the courage he could never will himself to have. Paris, in essence, becomes "fearless" as he becomes more like Fearless Jones. This transformation comes primarily through Paris rejecting a strictly self-defined, intellectual view of the self in favor of an identity that embraces the feelings of the "heart," including loyalty, love, and loss.

Mosley first introduces his readers to Fearless and Paris during a brief exchange in *Bad Boy Brawley Brown,* and Easy Rawlins mentions Paris's bookstore in *Little Scarlet*. After this first novel, *Fearless Jones,* Mosley revisits Paris and Fearless in two additional stories—*Fear Itself* (2003) and *Fear of the Dark* (2006).

Fearless Jones, set in 1954 Watts, opens with Paris happily—and generally without incident—operating a used bookstore that has been open for about a month. This peaceful bliss is interrupted, however, when Elana Love enters his store claiming to be looking for the Messenger of the Divine Church. She is followed closely by her brutal ex-boyfriend Leon, who beats Paris. Paris agrees to help Elana Love, and she tells him that Leon is after her because he thinks she has a bond that Leon got from his former cellmate, Sol Tanenbaum. Elana says, though, that she gave the bond to Reverend William Grove, a leader in the Messenger of the Divine Church. Elana then seduces Paris, steals his car and gun, and disappears.

Paris makes his way back to his store only to discover that it has been destroyed by an arsonist. Desperate to protect himself from further harm and to avenge his lost store, Paris decides to spring his best friend, Tristan "Fearless" Jones, from prison. Fearless and Paris begin their investigation with Sol Tanenbaum, but, when they arrive at his home, they find him beaten, stabbed, and near death. Sol's wife, Fanny, befriends the two men and takes them into her home as they continue to look for the men who tried to kill Sol over the bond.

Under the scrutiny of the seemingly unscrupulous detective Bernard Latham, the two men use clues from Elana's apartment and their community contacts to learn more about Elana, the Messenger of the Divine Church, and Reverend Grove. Their inquiries become more urgent and intense, however, after Fanny is murdered. When the men finally make contact with Reverend Grove, he asserts that Elana and Leon are the masterminds behind the bond scheme. Paris and Fearless's lawyer/bail bondsman friend Milo Sweet ties Leon to mob lawyers and, believing the bond to be potentially worth millions, offers to help the men solve their mystery in exchange for an equal cut of whatever money they get out of it. A fellow bail bondsman helps the team find Leon and Elana. Elana then explains how she and Leon planned to give the bond to a man who claimed he could use it to track down even more money. Fearless fights Leon and takes the bond.

As Paris, Fearless, and Elana travel across town in separate cars to meet Milo, Fearless and Elana are intercepted by Latham, who takes the young woman to a Beverly Hills hotel to meet with a mysterious white man, later revealed to be an Israeli government operative. Grove and Latham are also murdered soon after. The pieces of the mystery finally come together, though, when Fanny and Sol's nephew, Morris, kills himself and leaves a suicide note detailing how he strangled Fanny when she threatened to "raise hell" after he confessed his connections to Zev Minor, also known as Zimmerman, a Nazi war criminal (289).[2] Paris then surmises that Grove must have come into contact with Zimmerman, who plotted with Leon to get to Sol. After Sol dies in the hospital, Paris and Fearless find the Israeli secret-service agents and agree to help them locate Zimmerman, but Paris takes a detour to interview Theodore Wally, a former clerk at the grocery next to what was Paris's bookstore. Wally confesses to burning the store, explaining that the grocer wanted the bookstore's lot.

Fearless stops Paris from killing Wally, and the pair return to Milo's office, where they prepare for a meeting that Milo has set up with Zimmerman and his associates, including Leon. The tense meeting turns violent when the villains begin shooting each other after the Nazis refuse to stop speaking German. Milo and Fearless, caught in the crossfire, are shot in the arm and hand, respectively, but nevertheless escape. Paris, however, is arrested because the police suspect him of burning down his store. After weeks lost in the system with only an inept public defender to help him, he is released. Fearless arrives at the jail in a new car and explains how Sol revealed where to find the money he'd stashed away in international banks for his niece Gella, and how Gella had shared a "finder's fee" with her new friends (336).

Paris narrates all of the action, and Fearless is not even mentioned in the text until page 3; nor does he actually appear until over 40 pages into the text. Yet, as the novel's title would suggest, Fearless—specifically Paris's reflections on Fearless's characteristics, behaviors, and motivations—dominates the story. This imbalance suggests that Paris still struggles with self-definition and therefore seeks to find this definition vicariously by trying to better understand his antithesis.

Paris's descriptions of Fearless are frequent, elaborate, and vivid. Physically, Paris tells us, Fearless is "tall, over six feet, and though he's slender, his shoulders warn you about his strength. He's also a good looking man" with "a friendly face, a pleasant openness that makes you feel good" (48) and "a perpetual grin on his face" (52). He is "darker than most Negros in the American melting pot, he was stronger than tempered steel and an army-trained killing machine" (31). Paris then clarifies, "But for all that he was a killer, Fearless was a good man too. Too good. He was generous beyond his means" (32).

Intellectually, Paris explains, "Fearless wasn't a bright man, at least not in straightforward thinking. He only read at a sixth-grade level even though he finished high school. A child could beat him at checkers two times out of three" (42). He notes, however, that "Fearless had a smart heart. He had a brave heart too" (167); "he could survive in the harshest of environments" because of this ability to read and assess people and situations: "He could tell you if a man was going to pull out a gun or cry. You could fool Fearless sometimes, but he always seemed to make the right choices when the chips were down. And he had eyes in the back of his head" (42). Yet, "the best thing about Fearless," in Paris's evaluation, "was the attribute he was named for; he didn't fear anything, not death or pain or any kind of passion" (42). In one of his earliest descriptions, Paris says, "Fearless was the kind of person who attacked trouble. He didn't know how to look away or back down. He couldn't even spell the word *compromise*" (13).

Fearless also knows his own nature. Paris recounts that "Fearless considered himself and maybe three other people he's ever met to be *full bad*"; among those three others is Easy Rawlins's best friend, Raymond Alexander (176). He is also "a natural born anarchist. If he had what he needed, he thought of himself as a rich man; if he has less, well, that would have to do" (230). In this way, critic Jerrilyn McGregor argues, "While Fearless seemingly conforms to the brutal aspects of the badman, his construction of self moves beyond simply retaliatory acts by privileging feeling"; he "manages to transcend boundaries, but he is also governed by a clear, if unconventional, code of ethics."[3] He knows know that he is capable of violence, so he tries to live simply, appreciating the community and the quintessential joys, such as love and friendship.

Paris, in contrast, offers only very few and generally mundane descriptions of himself. He is "small and weak," (41) "five eight and slim" (48). He calls himself "a bookseller by trade, and a bookworm by nature" (279–280). Beyond this, he simply claims that "I was no hero but I was stubborn" (117) and that at the time of the story's action he was "a young fool" (191). His language only becomes more figurative and colorful when he describes his cowardice: "[. . .] I sat there trying to will myself up the evolutionary ladder from man to superman. But when I got out of that car, there was no cape dragging behind me, only a tail between my legs" (126). He knows his flaws enough to describe them with metaphor, but rather than explain or defend them, he mocks himself.

Paris also uses direct comparisons, or dichotomies, of himself and Fearless that are as much about who/what Paris is not as about who/what Fearless is. For example, early in the novel, as he and Elana flee Leon, Paris realizes, "If I were Fearless Jones I would have run headlong into the fray, taking blows and doing anything to protect her" (19). He also explains that "[Fearless's] generosity often led to trouble that I got pulled into. [. . .] And I am not a courageous man" (32). Because of this cowardice, Paris laments as he is waiting for Fearless at the jail, "Fearless was more free in that iron cage than I could ever be, on the outside" (46). Later, he adds, "On my own I watched or lied or misrepresented. I never took danger head-on if there was a second choice. Fearless was the opposite of me; he moved ahead as a rule. He might use a back entrance or even surprise, but no matter what, he was always going forward" (194). Paris sees his flaws clearly, but only because they contrast with Fearless's virtues.

Paris also explains, "I felt confident when Fearless was at my back, smart too" (171), suggesting that the relationship is both emotionally and intellectually stimulating. Yet, Paris's decision to separate himself from Fearless is based entirely on the rational decision that doing so would be better for the bookstore: "To protect my interests as a businessman, I decided to cut my ties with probably the best friend that I ever had" (13). Paris suggests that his bookstore is important not only because of his own investment, but also because "most black migrants from the South usually got jobs for the city or did domestic work or day labor. There were few entrepreneurs active among us at that time" (2). The bookstore is an opportunity for Paris to become a community leader and do grassroots work for racial uplift. The book business also suits Paris well early in the novel as he tries to distance himself from the emotional life that Fearless represents. Even when the cops question him about the origins of his books, he feels "no rancor toward them" because he rationalizes the harassment "by the law" as a kind of "a rite of passage for any Negro who wanted to better himself or his situation" (3).

This is not to say, though, that Paris does not have emotional moments before he meets Fearless or before Fearless comes into this particular story. But these moments generally revolve around the intellectual realm symbolized by books. Near the middle of the novel, Paris recalls his New Iberia, Louisiana, upbringing, which was defined by "one terrible event," that is, "learning to read" (122). Paris is especially scarred by a troubling encounter with a white librarian who tells him, "[. . .] no matter how much you know how to read, these books are not meant for you. These books were written by white people for white people. This is literature and art and the way our country is and should be" (124). The encounter—which *New York Times* critic Jesse Berrett parallels with Richard Wright's attempts to access his local library[4]—leaves young Paris distraught and aimless and undoubtedly lays the foundation for his equating the bookstore with personal and racial uplift later in his life.

Therefore, when the bookstore burns, Paris relives this childhood devastation. Upon finding the store destroyed, Paris "wept like a child. The tears ran down my cheeks, and my hands hung down. I stood there in the middle of the blackened lot that had been my future, quivering from the diaphragm" (35). He pines, "The bookstore was what made me somebody rather than just anybody" (41). Paris has imbued the bookstore, a seemingly intellectual endeavor, with such intense emotional weight that he equates the loss of the store with the loss of his personal and communal identities. The physical reaction to this loss reads more like a death than an arson. Indeed, since the fire does push Paris, albeit unwillingly, to liberate Fearless and begin a new journey toward a more complete, more balanced self, he is metaphorically resurrected from the books' ashes.

Paris foreshadows this resurrection early in the novel when he recounts a dream in which "someone was chasing me through the main library downtown"; in the dream, he narrates, "I ran from room to room with my unknown pursuer close behind. I knew that in one of the books was written the secret of my success and salvation, but I couldn't stop to search for it for fear that I'd get caught [. . .]" (33). Paris's fear keeps him from the knowledge that will save him, but ironically, he has this fear because of his overdependence on only one type of knowledge—the knowledge of the mind. He is surrounded and haunted by unknowns because he does not have the emotional maturity to "read" his situation and face it courageously.

Fearless, in contrast, not only knows no fear, but also understands the emotional roots of that fearlessness. He tells Paris simply, "Man wanna kill me or put me in prison, he's welcome to try it. But, you know, I draw from a deep well, deep as a muthafuckah" (116). He also "reads" even emotionally charged situations with surprising clarity. After Paris bails him out of jail, for example, Fearless says "in an usually sober tone," absent anger or malice, "I know you need me, Paris[. . . .] And whatever it is I'm 'onna help ya. 'Cause you know I got it" (49).

Paris admits that there was "no kindness" in his decision to pay for Fearless's release; he needed Fearless's "protection and particular brand of smarts" (42). Fearless's clarity and grace, though, move Paris to admit, "I was the one who was wrong. He proved that by forgiving me" (50).

Fearless's depth, clarity, and grace come from his privileging of humanity and emotional connections over selfish needs or pride. Fearless forges immediate, significant bonds with nearly everyone he meets, even the vicious dog he names Blood (78). Paris realizes that Fearless is "capable of murder," and he muses, "Even though I'm often frightened, I have never been afraid of Fearless. I felt such a deep kinship with him that he never scared me" (156), and he feels like he has known Fearless since childhood (3). Paris may be unsure of himself, but he is sure of Fearless. Paris, if only subconsciously, understands that Fearless's potential for violence will be unleashed only when Fearless needs to protect someone—especially someone like Paris, with whom he has an emotional connection, the same connection that Paris takes for granted. And to develop these meaningful connections, Fearless explains, "I listened to a lot of dyin' men, Paris. The trick is you got to keep your heart open. You got to listen wit' your heart" (226). Paris may see the value of the connection, but he is missing the ability to listen that would allow him to forge them with others. He has these bonds with Fearless because he listens to him—even though the motivation for doing so is initially selfish.

Fearless's understanding of and his willing to connect to the emotional roots of humanity do not, however, make him one-dimensional: he is not anti-intellectual or incapable of logical thinking. Seemingly following Paris's lead, some critics also describe Fearless and Paris as near-binaries. Richard Bernstein, for example, calls Fearless "unintellectual as Paris is geekish, and as two-fisted as Paris is not."[5] Fearless may not be "interested in [Paris's] puzzler's mind" (292), but in addition to his "particular brand of smarts," he also shows that he's more aware of nuance than Paris gives him credit for (43). For example, as they are leaving the novel's final shootout, Fearless insists that they find his lost finger. When Paris seems confused about why, Fearless reminds him that the finger has a "fingerprint on it" that could tie him to the crime scene (322). This intellectual clarity, even in a high-pressure situation, demonstrates when Fearless is emotional in other situations it is because he chooses to privilege the emotional; it is not merely a fall-back to make up for intellectual deficiency.

So, as Paris and Fearless work together to find Sol's bond and Fanny's killer, Paris changes dramatically as he observes, comments on, and is therefore shaped by Fearless's emotional-intellectual balance. This change is especially evident in his reaction to Fanny's death. Paris laments, "As I said before, I've been around hard times, but the death of that tiny woman who had taken me in without the slightest hesitation hit me hard. It was like I was groggy or something" (139). He later explains in more detail: "She was just an old white woman, that's what I thought, but she reminded me of the women in my own family. She was strong and brave in the face of people much more powerful than she." (154). Paris mourns for the loss of redemptive humanity that Fanny represented. Like Fearless, her aid is selfless and unqualified, even though he initially dismissed and misjudged her based on the *logic* that a white woman would never treat a black man with kindness. Her fearlessness, though, reminds him of his emotional past and thus evokes powerful and transformative emotion in him.

This reaction to Fanny's death also highlights the ways in which the text makes Paris's evolving emotional identity contingent upon his growing understanding of the similar racisms that inform both anti-Semitism and anti-black sentiment. At Sol and Fanny's house, Paris reads *Dead Souls* by Nikolai Gogol, who "wrote about the travesty of serfdom in old Russia," and he begins to think, "it seemed like those old white people used to own each other at the same time that whites owned blacks in America" (155). He again sees this link between black and Jewish oppression when the detective investigating Fanny's death asks Paris if Morris or Gella "might have wanted the old Jews harmed," and Paris realizes "*Jew* turned to *nigger* in my ears" (161). The link, and the fact that Paris comes to it through reading—his primary emotional vehicle— helps Paris merge his intellectual and emotional responses to Sol and Fanny's plight.

Fearless also understands this link because of his experiences as a soldier in World War II. Paris explains, "No black man liked the notion of concentration camps; we have lived in labor camps the first 250 years of our residence in America. And for Fearless it was even worse; he had actually seen the camps" (290–91). For Fearless, though, this compounded emotional experience, combined with his intolerance for injustice, is enough to form his singular motivation for solving the case. He declares near the end of the novel, "We want the dude caused it all; we want him to pay for what he did. Money's nice—we could all use some, I'm sure—but this is about making the traitor Jew pay for what he did" (302). In order for Paris to feel a connection to Fanny, he needs to have a link with her and her people that resonates comparatively with something in him—he needs a logical connection between the Jewish people and himself or his people. Fearless, though, can create an even stronger motivation based on simply observing the other's trauma.

The changes become more profound in the aftermath of Fanny's death and as the bodies and injustices continue to pile up. Paris lays out the facts of the case so far to Milo: "So you see," I explained, " I didn't start nuthin'. I mean, a man got to seek out some justice if he been done wrong, right?" (188). He starts to feel compelled to face his fears and stand up for others. Then, when he has to follow Latham, he successfully articulates a fear, confronts it, and overcomes it. He explains: "I've never respected law enforcement, merely feared it. I'm an honest man as far as it goes, meaning that I rather make my own money than take somebody else's. I'm almost always on the right side of the law, but law men scare me anyway, they terrify me. I have always believed that more black folks have been killed by those claiming to be enforcing the law than by those who were breaking it. So following that man I felt like a deer stalking a tiger, or a leaf pretending that it was driving the wind" (210). Paris is scared, and he even has reason to be scared. But he pushes through and acts anyway, despite the odds being out of his favor, because he knows it is what he has to do to pursue justice and protect his friends.

The fear still has the power to paralyze him, though, especially in situations that create emotional disconnection for him. After leaving Reverend Grove's funeral, for example, Paris recalls, "I took in great gulps of air, trying to bring my spirit back into alignment with my body—because that's how it felt, as if my soul were somehow trying to flee the flesh" (254). Paris feels the separation that fear creates; he feels his soul, the center of emotion, trying to break away from the rest of himself—body and mind. He considers further, "That's how it goes with me. I face danger and survive it, acting just fine, but as soon as it's over and I'm alone, I break down" (254). When he's alone—that is, without

Fearless—he loses any courage that he gained when he was with his friend and therefore a more complete and more balanced version of himself.

Fearless then explains to him that fear, on its own, is an emotion that can be distinct from cowardice; what a man does with that fear is what defines him as a coward or a hero. After Sol dies, when Fearless wants to continue to search for Sol and Fanny's killer, Paris and Fearless have the following exchange:

> "[. . .] I'm scared, man, scared to death with all these men fightin' and kil-lin'." The truth came out of me without my intention.
>
> Fearless put his steely hand on my shoulder.
>
> "You scared, but you ain't no coward, Paris. Uh-uh. Matter 'a fact, you a hero."
>
> "What?" I never knew Fearless to try and play anybody, much less me, his best friend. "Yeah. Hero is just bein' brave when there's trouble. An' bein' brave means to face your fears and do it anyway. Shoot. You can't call me a hero 'cause I ain't scared 'a nuthin' on God's blue Earth." (266)

Paris understands this distinction more clearly after the violent, nearly mur-derous, exchange he has with Theodore Wally when he confesses to burning down the bookstore. Paris explains, "I had almost killed Theodore, and that frightened me. I never believed it when people said that they lost control, that they blacked out like Morris said and killed without volition. Until that very moment I believed that the man made his own decisions, excuse of passion was just a lawyer's lie" (311). Before this event, Paris does not believe that the emotional and intellectual can be completely separate. Paris was not afraid in the moment, when his blind rage over the loss of his bookstore—his emotional locus—takes over; rather, he is afraid *after* the loss of control when he tries to think rationally, or intellectually, about his actions.

At the end of the story, Paris emerges from his prison cell a new man. In a clear reversal of the narrative, Fearless picks up Paris from jail after working with Milo to get him released. The last paragraph then looks ahead to an inde-terminate point in the future in which Paris has a steady girlfriend and has as-sumed the role of Fearless's protector: "[Fearless] hasn't gotten in any trouble, and I'm hoping that he doesn't. But I know that if he does, I'll have to help him, because Fearless is my friend" (337). This resolution is a dramatic shift from the meek Paris who opened the novel. Paris makes an unconditional commitment to be Fearless's companion and savior. No longer a coward, he has become the fearless friend he always wanted to be.

CHAPTER FOUR

New York, New History, New Detective
The Long Fall

Walter Mosley's "junior" detective is a former aspiring boxer turned Buddhist, the orphaned son of an ardent Communist. Leonid Trotter "LT" McGill lives in post-9/11 New York City and relies heavily on technology in his investigations. Leonid, a licensed private detective, spent most of his life working outside the law, doing favors and orchestrating elaborate setups for the mob and other nefarious characters, but he tries to change his ways after the daughter of one of his victims exacts an emotional revenge on him.

Leonid—like Easy Rawlins, Fearless Jones, and Paris Minton—is a man of many vices; yet, like his "elders," he is also, fundamentally, a good man. Still, according to Mosley, Leonid "couldn't get more different from Easy Rawlins if you tried."[1] The most significant difference between Leonid and Mosley's previous detectives is that, primarily by virtue of his contemporary context, Leonid is not subject to the degree or myriad types of racism his predecessors experienced. Leonid himself observes: "This was the year 2008, and race, though still a major player in American culture, had undergone a serious transmogrification. A black man was running for president. There was a legally blind black man in the governor's seat in Albany. White American children and adults had heroes from Snoop Dogg to Tiger Woods. This wasn't the age of being pushed to the back of the bus or excluded from the awareness of the media" (170).[2]

This shift, though, does not mean that race has disappeared from the new detective's stories; on the contrary, Oline Codgill asserts in a review of *The Long Fall*, "A hallmark of Mosley's novels is his view of race and class and he succinctly shows how some things have changed since Easy's times, while other facets remain the same."[3] So, Leonid's stories still consider the impact of twenty-first-century discourse about race and ethnicity, but race is not central to those stories. Mosley has said of Leonid, "There are still times he walks into a room that defines him by his race, but his world is much more complex, in some ways, than Easy's or Fearless's"; he adds, "It's a new world. There's an awareness of race now, but there's not the overpowering dominance of race that you had in the 20th century."[4]

Leonid, for example, describes being "profiled," but he attributes the experience to his demeanor rather than his race. He explains, "I was selected for extra security measures at the airport checkpoint and studied by a series of dogs, machines, and Homeland Security experts with six weeks' training [. . .] probably because of something in my attitude. Maybe they can sense the rage in me." (79). He also observes, "It wasn't 2008 everywhere in America. Some people still lived in the sixties, and others might as well have been veterans of the Civil War" (84). Later, when a suspect tries to shake him with racist language, Leonid simply thinks to himself, "If we were in Missouri sometime before 1980 he might have riled me some" (306). But in twenty-first-century New York City, this single sentence is all the reaction the epithet inspires.

Without this stifling backdrop of unrelenting racist oppression, Leonid is freer to shift his focus to the complex relationship between present-day social dilemmas and the personal as well as the communal past, and the stories are free to devote more time to metafictional elements. Specifically, ruminations on post-9/11 New York life and expanded personal and familial story lines dominate Leonid's novels. These story lines are then complemented by commentary on detective fiction and detective craft.

Although race does not affect Leonid as immediately and profoundly, his world and his experiences are far from "post-racial." As Mosley asserts, "How can we say we live in a post-racial world, as if we didn't have millions of black men in prison . . . as if people of color weren't still facing this economic divide." For Mosley, the racialized world has simply expanded: "I have a story that I tell: about how, in the 20th century, a young black man in Detroit would say, 'It's tough on a young black man in Detroit,' and I would be saying, 'I know what you're talking about, brother,' and in the early 21st century, you could go there, and ask 'How ya doing?,' and he'd say, 'I'm OK, but it's hard on a young black man in Detroit,' and I'd say 'I know, brother, but the world is so big—there is a guy in Kandahar who would be happy to trade apartments with us.'"[5] Race still matters, but race is just one element in a larger global conversation about oppression and privilege.

The first four novels in the ongoing series—*The Long Fall* (2009), *Known to Evil* (2010), *When the Thrill Is Gone* (2011), and *All I Did Was Shoot My*

Man (2012)—each generally follow a three-plot structure. One plot centers on a client whose case Leonid is being paid to investigate, the second on a drama within Leonid's family, and the third on a person or situation from Leonid's sordid past, which he has left behind just over a year and a half before the events in *The Long Fall* (34). None of these plots is a subplot to the others; all are equally developed and fully engaging for Leonid, and all devote significant space to Leonid's reflections on post-9/11 New York and exploration of personal and communal identities as well as to the novels' metafictional nods. Examining the first novel, *The Long Fall*, in detail provides an entry point and model for understanding the rest of this series.

In *The Long Fall*, a mysterious man named Ambrose Thurman hires Leonid to find four men for Thurman's anonymous employer, who only knows their childhood nicknames. Leonid uses one of his many semi-honest contacts to locate the young men and reluctantly turns over their names to the dodgy Thurman. Not long after, one of the men turns up dead. Troubled by his potential complicity in the murder, Leonid flies to Albany to track down Thurman and the truth. There, however, he finds that Thurman, whose real name is Norman Fell, has been killed as well. Leonid returns to New York to learn that yet another man on the list has been murdered.

When professional assassin Willie Sanderson also attempts to kill Leonid, he subdues the giant and the police capture him. Sanderson will not reveal his employer, though, so Leonid continues to investigate. With the help of inside man Alphonse Renaldo, Leonid interviews William Nilson, also known as Toolie, the only man from Thurman's list who is still alive, despite being stabbed in jail. Toolie details the events leading to the accidental death of Thom Paxton, also known as Smiles, a white kid who ran with the list crew. Leonid builds relationships in the Albany criminal community and then uses these connections to investigate Sanderson, who he traces to the Sunset Sanatorium where he was first a patient, then an orderly, and where he continues to develop an already existing relationship with Bunny Hull.

As Leonid explores the relationship between Sanderson and the Hulls, he develops a friendship with young coed Hannah Hull. Leonid then foils the plans of another would-be assassin, who fingers Roman Hull as the man who hired him. When Leonid confronts the bedridden "octogenarian" about why he tried to kill him, the patriarch simply tells him that it was "family business" (307). Sanderson escapes from the hospital, and thinking that Bunny has betrayed him, heads to the Hull house to kill her. Leonid rushes to the house, where he finds Sanderson choking Hannah. The two fight again, and Leonid kills him. Kitteridge later reveals that Thom Paxton was Bunny's son and that she hired Sanderson to avenge his death.

Meanwhile, ever suspicious of his too-smart son Twill's semi-criminal activities, Leonid—with the help of his personal hacker, Tiny "Bug" Bateman—has been "shadowing" Twill's online activity. Leonid becomes especially concerned, though, when he discovers correspondence between Twill and a girl, later revealed to be Mardi Bitterman, who wants to kill her father herself, but Twill offers to "take care of it" instead. So, Leonid begins investigating Mardi's father, Leslie. When he poses as a repair man to get access to the Bitterman house and then hacks into Leslie's computer, he finds the reason for Mardi's desperation: "there were well over a thousand photographs of a naked man and child in the most depraved positions. The girl in the photographs ranged in age from eight to about twelve, before puberty began to rear its hormones. Sometime she was smiling, sometime she cried, open mouth and in despair. The man had a stern look and was always erect" (238). Leonid then convinces Mardi to reveals the details of Twill's plot to kill Leslie, and Leonid intervenes just in time to stop him. Leonid then sets up a fake pornography site linked to Leslie and gives the information about this site to Carson Kitteridge.

At the same time, Tony "The Suit" Towers, one of Leonid's former gangster associates, asks Leonid to look for a man named A. Mann, who Tony claims was his "personal accountant" during a period that the IRS is now investigating Tony's finances for. (64). Leonid does not believe him, but he knows that he does not really have a choice about whether to help Tony: "The moment I turned over Mann's address, he and the dog would be dead. If I refused to turn the name over, I'd be on Tony's blacklist and someone else would root out the accountant. The odds between me and Tony were pretty much even but if Harris Vartan decided to weigh in on the gangster's side I wouldn't make it a day. I didn't have much of a choice, and I had a family that needed me breathing in order for them to stay afloat" (181–82). Leonid does give Mann's information to Tony, but when he arrives to kill Mann, federal agents are waiting to take Tony to jail and Mann to witness protection.

It is within the context of the second plot in general and in Leonid's observations on Twill specifically that the reader is first introduced to the New York elements of Leonid's story. The focus on New York is significant because it is, literally, on the other side of the country from Los Angeles—Mosley's birthplace and the setting for both the Easy Rawlins and the Fearless Jones stories—and because New York City is Mosley's current home. Mosley explains, "The reason I wrote Easy Rawlins was something I felt I owed to my family and my father. There was so much about our history, black men's history especially, that is left out of the literature and in non-fiction," but with Leonid McGill, he continues, "I'm actually writing about myself and my world. And Leonid reflects me and my world much more than Easy does. And it was time to come into the present." Mosley also claims that, "as we turn into the new century, New York has a lot to do with what is happening in the world. And writing about Leonid . . . it's time to write about New York."[6] Leonid's stories demonstrate how—in the wake of the 9/11 terror attacks—New York becomes a locus for discourse on violence, healing, and race in national and global contexts.

Leonid clearly loves New York. He walks most places, even when they are far enough away that he could justify taking a taxi, and he realizes that he has almost blinding pride in the city: "sometimes being a New Yorker brought on the feeling of false superiority that made me slip up badly" (210). This "superiority" seems to stem from the fact that Leonid equates New York and its post-9/11 recovery with strength, integrity, and community. These sentiments emerge most obviously when Leonid links memories of the terror attacks to thoughts of his son Twill. While walking home one evening, Leonid muses:

> Gazing at the gap in the skyline left by the World Trade Center, I thought about Twill. Not of my blood, he was tall and lithe, handsome and quick to smile. The only thing we had somewhat in common was our dark coloring but even there our skins were different hues. I had more brown to my blackness. But blood relations are overrated. Twill had a way of making you feel good. His greeting—morning or night being picked up at the police station or after school function—was always friendly and sincere. His head was cool and his heart warm. And so it was my self appointed duty to make sure that he wasn't pulled down in the wake of his own superiority. (27)

Twill, whom Leonid later calls "a perfect person" because of his unwavering and unselfish commitment to making sensible and just decisions with no regard for "consequences" (241), is also Mosley's "best" and "favorite character that [he has] ever written."[7] Twill is not Leonid's biological son, but the adopted father nevertheless feels a particular kinship with the boy that is born not from race or even shared blood, but instead from shared experiences and shared admiration. Leonid loves Twill and New York because of the deep, fulfilling, and nearly indescribable connections that he feels with both and because both link him to a communal justice and kinship that transcend race.

As Leonid rides the subway, he realizes, "the only city I could live in is New York. Most other American municipalities are segregated by class and culture, education and personal choice"; in New York, though, "everybody is jumbled up together and bounced around until you have African princes walking side by side with Appalachian Daughters of the American Revolution, and aspiring starlets making room for hopeful housewives past their prime" (167). Leonid also feels an almost magnetic attraction to Lower Manhattan, ground zero of the 9/11 attacks. He observes, "With the police knocking on my door, dead men in my wake, killers studying my name, I knew that I had to get my butt in gear and head way downtown, where the laws of nature and the laws of man intersect, intertwine, and make up a whole new system of justice" (166). Since 9/11's violence made New York a discursive center, ground zero is the center of the center—the epicenter—where the energy converges and intensifies. For Leonid this intensity helps him make sense of the personal violence that pursues him.

While Leonid can self-identify as a New Yorker—a geographic rather than a racial marker—he also sees that the city nevertheless has the potential to inflict its own terrors through deeply oppressive power structures. These structures show up most obviously in the New York City Police Department and in nebulously powerful Alfonse Rinaldo, "Special Assistant to the City of New York."

Crooked cops are not unique to the Leonid stories, of course. Most of Mosley's characters are, to some extent, suspicious of the police. Leonid's suspicions stem from what he sees as the police force's need to harass and intimidate without remorse or recourse. He asserts, "The police love it when a suspect, or just somebody they don't like, is feeling uncomfortable. It doesn't matter if that person of interest is innocent and doesn't deserve the abuse. [. . .] Their job is to make people like me feel nauseous and angst-ridden" (157). Since these sentiments mirror those that Easy Rawlins expressed about most of the policemen he met in the decades his narratives cover, Leonid's experiences with the police suggest that not even the transformative violence of 9/11 could subvert the power-lust that leads people with authority to bully anyone—regardless of race—they see as a threat to that authority.

Leonid's communal and redemptive vision of New York is also complicated by the "Important Man," Alphonse Rinaldo (169). Rinaldo is a seemingly omnipotent and omniscient power broker with seemingly endless secret political and social connections. In the days before he tried to set his life straight, Leonid helped Rinaldo with a "favor," so the detective earned a convenient ally. Leonid observes that Rinaldo "might have seemed to be of a mild temper, but many of the worst monsters I've known were like that: pleasant even in the regrettable act of murder" (173).

Leonid remembers asking "Rinaldo if he answered directly to the mayor"; Rinaldo replied, "'I am the special assistant to the City of New York,' [. . .] as if there were a grim god that lived under the stone and steel, concrete and grim, of the city, a god whose will carried more weight than any politician or generation of voters" (173). In Rinaldo, Leonid sees New York's "underworld" of oppressive possibilities. Rinaldo does not answer to a specific person or power in the city; he answers to the city itself, suggesting the city's potential for evil and subterfuge. Leonid does, in fact, imagine that Rinaldo's power comes from the spirit of New York. He posits, "if Manhattan was an ancient deity set to oversee our island and its neighbors, then Alphonse Rinaldo was an errant angel thrown down among swine"; like Satan, "he could buy your soul from a third party and send it twirling like a glass top on the granite stairs of justice. He was without peer, the most dangerous man in New York City. He almost always knew more than anyone else in the room" (174). The god(s) that created and control Rinaldo are omnipresent—both above and below the city. And while Rinaldo is a fallen angel, with all the evil possibilities that implies, these god(s) have nevertheless allowed him to retain near omniscience about and omnipotence over human affairs. Leonid needs Rinaldo to solve his mysteries, and Rinaldo knows this, so both the need and the knowledge give him power.

As Leonid leaves Rinaldo's office, the white man observes that Leonid and Rinaldo's assistant, Christian, "are the only two black men, American-born black men, that have ever been in this office," and he asks, "Do you find that strange?" Leonid responds simply, "Only thing strange is that you realize it" (176). Leonid's surprise at the white man's hyperawareness of race suggests either that Leonid himself would not have realized it or that he would expect Rinaldo to be so blinded by white privilege that he would not even *see* Leonid's race (as was the case with Easy Rawlins and Todd Carter in *Devil in Blue Dress*). In both cases, the novel takes the responsibility for racial consciousness away from the black characters and shifts it onto the white.

The shift away from the omnipresent racial concerns do not, however, mean that Leonid has forgotten the past. On the contrary, Leonid's personal history in general—and in particular, his patriarchal communist upbringing and his need to atone for his semi-criminal life—play an integral role in each text's complicated plot sequence. The title of the novel underscores this integral role. "The Long Fall" refers to the end of Leonid's recurring dream about falling from a burning building. Although the dream varies in its minute details, it always involves fire and falling. The first dream Leonid recounts begins with him "running through a maze of blazing hallways"; to escape, he breaks through a window: "As the window falls I am faced with the most beautiful blue sky I have ever seen. Below, the broken pane and flaming timbers are still falling through thousands of feet to earth. Fire and heat pulse behind me. The day beckons. The wind is bracing, and the choice . . . no choice at all" (55). The final image before he awakens is "the ground [. . .] racing toward me with deadly indifference" (55).

Since Leonid is both literally and metaphorically running from his past in the novel, the flames suggest the damnation that he narrowly avoided by leaving his life of almost-crime. While the limited options for escape and the free fall point to an unexpected lack of control in his new life, the beauty of the fall, even of the gravity that pulls him to the ground, is comforting—until he realizes that it will inevitably end in his death. This violent collision parallels the sometimes violent intersection between his past and present, as well as his personal and professional lives.

Almost all of the powerful figures from Leonid's past are white, which when combined with the lack of choices that Leonid has vis-à-vis these white men, suggests that his escape from crime was a grander social gesture rather than merely an isolated individual choice. This is emphasized by his discussions of his past or people from his past being characterized by a passivity or lack of choice, whereas his "new life" is characterized by active, deliberate action. Early in the text, Leonid tells boxing coach/mentor Gordo, "'Let's just say I realized that I've done some things wrong,' I said. 'I'm tryin' to backtrack now [. . .] trying to make right what I can'" (11). Leonid is actively trying to move in a different direction, to right wrongs, to start on a new path—just like his actively pushing out the window in the burning building in his dream. But when Tony the Suit comes to Leonid's office, Leonid considers action, yet ultimately does nothing. He reports, "I considered asking him his business right there in the hall, telling him without uttering the words that he was no longer welcome in my world. But pushing Tony Towers away would be like sweeping a rattlesnake under the bed before retiring" (61). Leonid attributes his lack of action to powerlessness: "since I had vacated my position as a PI for the various mobs and crews I have no natural defenses against men like him" (61). This powerlessness, through, mirrors the dream's free fall. He is no longer under the gangsters' direct control; he has escaped the life of crime that the fire symbolized, but he still has no choice, no control over his life after making this choice. There is no stopping gravity, just as there are "no natural defenses" against men like Tony.

Also, in making family more central to Leonid's story and by having the personal and professional spheres of Leonid's life not just converge but violently collide at times, the stories show that Leonid's detective work is not just about the cases he investigates; his work also shapes him and his understanding of his familial history while, in turn, his present-day family dramas and evolving understanding of his familial history—especially his relationship with his father—influence his understanding of his cases.

Comparing Easy Rawlins and Leonid McGill provides a helpful contrast. Easy, like Leonid, certainly loves his family, and his desire to protect and care for that family informs his decisions and even motivates him to improve himself and his situations. Also, Easy's friends, Raymond "Mouse" Alexander and Jackson Blue in particular, protect him and help him with his investigations, and they both have well-developed subplots in multiple mysteries, just like many of Leonid's friends. However, the dramas that involve Easy's wives/ girlfriends and children are at worst distractions, at best subplots, and always simply supplementary to his central story lines. Easy adopts both his son and his daughter because he is involved in investigating the events that leave both children orphaned; Easy's girlfriend even committed one of the murders Easy investigated. His dog, the title character in *A Little Yellow Dog*, actually has a much larger role in a story than any of Easy's family members.

Easy and Leonid both, however, have missing fathers, and while Easy does reflect at length about his father's life in the coming-of-age novel *Gone Fishin'* (1997), these reflections do not dominate Easy's mystery stories like they do Leonid's. Reflection on Leonid's father's "lessons" about politics, economics, and human nature color Leonid's own observations and investigations, but they are all tinged with bitterness: "Maybe if my father, Tolstoy McGill, hadn't gone off to South America to fight the fascists or the capitalists or whoever, maybe if he'd come back and been a parent to me, I would have tried to live by the vision of his perfect world. Maybe if my mother, once she knew the love of her life was never coming back, hadn't gone to her bed to lay there until the doctors came and took her off to the hospital to die, maybe then I would have taken a different path. [. . .] But as it was I had to make my own way in a world of chains and choking, imperfect choices and the fools who made them" (35).

The mysteries surrounding Tolstoy McGill—his whereabouts and his motivations (mysteries he actually solves in later texts)—are the core personal mystery in the novel, and while he works to solve the case he was hired to solve, he often finds himself reflecting on how Tolstoy's lessons shaped him and created the imperfections that led to his convoluted personal and professional boundaries.

These complicated boundaries and "imperfect choices," though, are an inevitable part of the detective's life. Early in the novel, Leonid works on a crossword puzzle. The last clue he completes before heading out to his office is "the five-letter name for 'Black crime writer,'" although he does not reveal his answer (57). This nod situates Leonid firmly in the African American mystery tradition. *USA Today*'s Carol Memmott calls Leonid "noir"—even more so than Easy[8]—and Mosley says Leonid is evoking a "really perfect hard-boiled character."[9] To underscore Leonid's place in this tradition, the text devotes time to reflecting on the craft of detective work. These reflections center on inquiry, logic, and human nature as on the role of these in discovering "truth," suggesting that Leonid may also be trying to unlock the mysteries of human nature in general—and the mysteries of his own life and nature specifically—while he unlocks the mystery of his specific case. Each time the text offers a reflection on the craft of detective work or the qualities of an ideal detective, it links this reflection with another key person, theme, or issue in Leonid's narrative.

For example, while looking for Ambrose Thurman in Albany, Leonid reflects on detective craft, starting as a parallel with police work and evolving into a boxing metaphor. He posits: "In some ways the objective of the private detective is similar to that of the beat cop. [. . .] You have to live completely in every moment, because if you get beyond yourself something will certainly blindside you and leave you face down in the street" (84). Just a few pages later, Leonid offers a related observation: "Being a boxer, even just an amateur like me, can make a man reckless" (86). By linking boxing and detective work, the text shows the centrality of both to Leonid's definition of himself. The connection also demonstrates how his job shapes and is shaped by his past, since boxing became the solace of his lonely childhood.

Similarly Leonid finds solace—this time from his unhappy marriage—in his relationship with Aura, the beautiful building manager he fell in love with after his wife, Katrina, left him for another man. Leonid felt compelled to take Katrina back when she asked for his forgiveness, though, and he was thus obligated to abandon his relationship with Aura. Aura nevertheless remains an important and rare confidant in his life. He reflects, "The first thing you learned in my line of business was that you never give up any information that you don't absolutely have to. Katrina knew nothing about my business. But Aura represented a whole new movement in my life. The time I spent with her was painfully honest" (115). This reflection show the toll that investigative work can take on a detective. In a profession based on lies and obfuscation, detectives can lose perspective on what is real versus what is fabricated. Katrina, who privileges wealth and image, personifies this fabrication, while Aura's genuine love for Leonid connects him to the honest world.

In addition to hiding the truth, the detective, Leonid reminds us, must sometimes hide himself. As he gives misinformation to the administrator at the Sunset Sanatorium, Leonid muses: "I find in my profession that it behooves one to appear ignorant, or, better yet, stupid, to the people you interrogate. It gives them a feeling of superiority, of having a mental leg up on you, so to speak" (207). This sentiment, like Leonid's reflections on Aura, reiterate the essential role of fabrication and subterfuge in the detective's craft. But with this nuanced description, the novel also evokes a link between Leonid's detective work and the masking tradition—represented most famously in Claude McKay's poem "We Wear the Mask"—in which African Americans pretend to be happy or ignorant to hide their true emotions from their white oppressors.

Leonid uses this masking to help his case, not just himself, and when he leaves Sunset, he removes his mask. Still, linking this rich African American cultural tradition with Leonid's detective work brings *The Long Fall*'s focus back to race, if only temporarily, and Leonid cannot possibly be a post-racial detective as long as he uses this tool. He does, however, have the freedom to put the mask away, drive back to New York, and focus on—instead of race—the other personal demons that wait for him there.

CHAPTER FIVE

Mysterious Genres
Narrative Fragmentation in *Blue Light* and *Diablerie*

When a writer has already found critical and popular success in a specific genre, critics and readers may struggle to embrace that author's moves into new genres. Walter Mosley, however, makes his move away from mystery easier on his fans and followers because the themes in his fiction in other genres overlap distinctly with those in his mystery fiction.

For example, Mosley's first science-fiction novel, *Blue Light* (1998)—which appeared just a year after the sixth Easy Rawlins novel—takes place in an alternate reality where race, class, and gender have the potential to be completely reimagined, yet are still subject to oppressive power dynamics. Even when characters are "enlightened" by a force such as the blue light, human nature still privileges the philosophies that divide in order to control—just as they do in Easy's Los Angeles. By investigating this alternate world, *Blue Light* asks readers to more closely examine the present world in general and its memories and representations of the past specifically.

Mosley's second book of erotica, *Diablerie* (2008)—which picks up the "sexistentialist" tropes he explored in *Killing Johnny Fry* (2008)—also asks readers to reconsider the dynamics of power and control, but in a more personal, even intimate, context. The protagonists in Mosley's erotica grapple with impulses they cannot fully understand, but ultimately they come to realize the transformative power of fear, rage, and sexuality. Fueled by betrayal, desire, and even bloodlust, *Diablerie's* morally ambiguous protagonist—who is reminiscent not only of Easy's best friend Raymond Alexander, but also of *The Man in My Basement*'s (2004) jaded host Charles Blakey—speeds toward a self-destruction that can only be mitigated by hard-won philosophical awakening.

Both novels' stories are thus mysteries in their own right. The protagonists in both must construct or reconstruct both personal and shared narratives in order to make sense of their situations and themselves. And as in many of Mosley's texts, regardless of genre, constructing or reconstructing that narrative is dependent on coming to terms with or understanding a racialized past. In *Blue Light,* understanding the narratives and solving the mystery depend on a reader's ability to embrace a nonlinear, fragmented view of history and identity. In *Diablerie,* the answer depends on finding redemption and self-fulfillment through meaningful connections with the past and future.

Blue Light

Set in and around San Francisco and Berkeley, California, *Blue Light* begins in and focuses primarily on events in 1969 but eventually covers more than twenty years. The novel opens with Lester "Chance" Foote, the narrator, recalling a sermon in which his mentor, Ordé, attempts to describe the origins of the blue light, a mystical force that grants its hosts unparalleled strength, knowledge, and vision. The text then explains how key characters each received the light on August 8, 1965: young Reggie Brown and his two-and-a-half-year-old twin sisters were standing on a street corner, and only the boy and one sister, Wanita, survived; the deranged Winch Fargo was robbing Eileen and Philip Martel of their church-bazaar earnings, and although Fargo shot the husband, it was the light that killed him; Claudia Zimmerman, with her dog looking on, was having an affair with her neighbor's husband in the backyard, and she ripped his nipple off with her teeth; Horace LaFontaine, dying of cancer, became an electrified zombie and inadvertently killed his brother-in-law with the combined force of the electricity and the blue light before wandering off into the desert; Ordé, the soon-to-be teacher-prophet, was sunbathing with his girlfriend Addy, who slept unaffected by the light's power.

Chance was not near anyone who received the blue light; he was trying to kill himself in a storage closet at the time. He later meets Ordé, who explains that the light affected Chance because of his vulnerability. Ordé convinces Chance to join his group of followers. Chance explains that the whole story is part of a documentary record, called *The History of the Coming of Light,* that he is writing in a wooden book, and he is able to tell everyone's story because he saw their memories during a blood-sharing ritual Ordé performed with him.

Ordé's church, the Close Congregation, meets Wednesdays in Berkeley's Graber Park and draws acolytes who have survived or been otherwise influenced by or drawn to the blue light. The followers who had direct contact with and survived the blue light come to be called "The Blues," whereas those who have heightened consciousness due to an indirect or partial contact with the blue light are called "half lights." Each of the Blues has a specific power—for example, Reggie finds, Eileen calms, Claudia seduces—and most of the Blues and half lights can sense each others' presence.

When Phyllis, one of the Blues, goes missing, Ordé becomes paranoid and distant. Reggie leads Chance to Phyllis's mutilated body, and Chance takes some of Phyllis's blood back to Ordé for the blood ritual, which reveals that Phyllis was killed by Death incarnate, also known as "The Gray Man," an evil force that has inhabited the resurrected body of Horace LaFontaine. The Gray Man, posing as a traveler named Gray Redstar, hunts the Blues, and when Addie resurfaces with her and Ordé's daughter, Julia "Alacrity," the first Blue born on Earth, the Gray Man immediately, but unsuccessfully, tries to attack the child. At the next congregation meeting, Ordé tells the group to disband, but before they can, the Gray Man appears and slaughters Ordé as well as many of the followers, including Eileen.

The survivors scatter. Claudia sets up her own congregation and breaks Winch Fargo out of prison to join her there. Chance, Addie, and the children flee together and seek refuge in the forests outside San Francisco. The Gray Man pursues the Blues, and even though he is weakened by an encounter with a redwood tree that has become a Blue, he tracks Winch Fargo, Claudia, and other Blues to Sacramento, where Claudia is jailed following a police raid on her congregation. Winch Fargo and the Gray Man fight; Winch loses an arm, and the Gray Man is so severely weakened that he must retreat to the desert to hibernate.

From their refuge in the woods, Chance and the others begin hearing and feeling a kind of musical call that they believe will lead them to safety. As they follow it, however, forest creatures—specifically butterflies and bears—begin to attack them. Nearly overpowered, they are rescued by Juan Thrombone ("Bones"), a Blue who cares for the forest and a settlement there called Treaty. Chance, Addie, and the children decide to stay there with Bones, and other Blues and half lights come to join them.

More than a decade later, the Gray Man awakens revitalized and makes his way to Treaty. Sensing and foreseeing Death's arrival, the Blues rename their "nation" War, send the half lights away, and prepare for battle. Many remain, though, and join the battle. Bones, with the help of the trees and the half lights, defeats Death, although he also perishes, and Chance helps everyone escape. Chance then loses consciousness. When he wakes up, he frantically searches for his friends, but they are gone. He passes out again, and this time wakes up in a straitjacket in the hospital, charged with starting the fire that ended the battle. When he tries to explain the Blues and the Gray Man, the doctors diagnose him with paranoid schizophrenia.

Blue Light's time line feels disjointed due, primarily, to the anachronistic reflections and dialogue that interrupt the central story and serve to show that Chance is recalling and writing from memory with significant distance from the actual time of the events. But this disorientation also creates a sense of fragmentation that reflects the fragmentation in Chance's identity, as well as the fragmentation in the blue light itself.

Chance devotes lengthy sections of his recollections to sermons and conversations focused on the nature of the blue light. The novel, in fact, opens with one such sermon, delivered by Ordé. Chance explains,

> *I didn't use a tape recorder back then, but I remember every word. Our teacher stood on a simple flat rock and told us about the blue light. What it meant—at least, as much as we could understand. Here is what he said:* [. . .] "I was once simple flesh like you, a man with meaningless words. But I was also a sleeping streak of blue light, scant seconds in length, jarred to consciousness after an age of silence. In the din of radiance rising from Neptune, I awoke and found myself leaning toward the cold gravity of that titan, rushing toward the small star it orbited. Ahead lay oblivion or the seed left on earth eons before and, hopefully, grown to stature." (3)[1]

Ordé describes joining with "other lights—exactly the same hue—at my side, each one a perfect array unwavering in its relationship to the rest. Each one made up of a flawless matrix of thought repeated again and again in a swirl of equations that held the secrets of your deepest dreams" (3). These lights joining together, though, "caused friction, squeals of false consciousness" (3), and many of the lights "died in the ecstasy you call the sun" (4). Nevertheless, "nearly 10,000 blue needles were destined to break the skin of air, their divine messages still intact" (4). The light is otherworldly and divine, and while it appears as just pieces of overwhelming knowledge, it still forges connections both among and within those it touches.

Near the end of the novel, Bones—who is notably less self-obsessed than Ordé but who is still, according to the dreamer Wanita, "all mixed up" from "too much blue in him" (210)—offers another perspective on the blue light. Chance asks Bones, "What is the blue light?" (215), and after explaining to Chance why he has asked the "wrong" question, Bones finally concludes:

> All the world is music, you see. There is music in atoms and music in suns. That is the range of the scale that you can see and read. There is music in emptiness and silence between. Everything is singing all the time, all the time. Singing and calling for what is missing. Your science calls it gravity. But the gods call it dance. They dance and fornicate; they listen and sing.

They call to distant flowers when buds ring out. Because, you see, it is not only atoms and suns that vibrate in tune. Rocks sing, as do water and air. The molecules that build blood and men also build the wasp; these too sing a minor note that travels throughout the stars. Greedy little ditties that repeat and repeat again and again the same silly melodies. (216–17)

For Bones, the light is a creative force, manifested in music, that reconciles god and science, nature and man.

Even those victims, such as Eileen's husband, Phillip, who do not survive the blue light's impact, still feel its positive, synthesizing enlightenment. As he dies, Phillip feels "sad for all those years before the light," but he also "felt a sudden awareness in a place so far away it was impossible to imagine. But he was there. Not him, Philip, but them—blue radiant spawn. Somehow their memories merged," and this merger helps him to be "transported so far away and long ago that he saw the birth of Earth in a pinwheel of self-knowledge" (8). He describes the experience as "the long journey home" and ultimately a oneness of existence as "his mind became part of the light as the light prepared to join the magnetic energy that flowed through the ground under his feet" (8). New York Times critic Mel Watkins links these features of Mosley's blue light to Ishmael Reed's "Jes Grew" in Mumbo Jumbo because the blue light "alludes to a spiritual power that transforms humans, freeing them from repression and unveiling the natural life force within. It is also driven by the magic of song and dance."[2]

Together, the three men's descriptions of the light and the Blues link both strongly to the blues aesthetic in African American art and culture. In his groundbreaking critical analysis Blues, Ideology, and Afro-American Literature, Houston A. Baker Jr. explains, "Afro-American culture is a complex, reflexive enterprise which finds its proper figuration in blues conceived as a matrix." Like the "flawless matrix" of blue light that Ordé describes, Baker explains, "the matrix is a womb, a network, a fossil-bearing rock. [. . .] The matrix is a point of ceaseless input and output, a web of intersecting impulses always in productive transit."[3] The blues aesthetic and the blue light connect as they undulate, unlocking creative potential.

This connection to the blues aesthetic also links Chance's experience, his narrative about the blue light, and the racialized trauma that made him initially susceptible to the blue light's influence. As Baker explains, "Rather than a rigidly personalized form, the blues offers a phylogenic recapitulation—a nonlinear, freely associative, nonsequential meditation—of species existence."[4] Chance's narrative form shares these characteristics with the blues aesthetic, making his history of the Blues also a blues history.

Chance longs to feel connections to the past and to be a part of a larger narrative than his own complicated personal history. During his failed graduate-school studies, Chance studied Thucydides because "the general and medical observer and historian not only told history but was himself a part of that history; he *was* history" (46). Chance's *History*, the written text and the book itself, then, becomes a record of his longing for this connection and his journey to find it.

Before Chance feels the blue light and meets Ordé, the *History* simply chronicles late-1960s counterculture. Chance explains: "It was a chronicle of the bay area at that time. Everyone back then felt the change in the air. It was the first time since the ancient city states that a city was the center of change for the whole world. I was going to document that change" (17). These changes, though, also create a context that obfuscates Chance's cultural isolation. "At any other time," he writes, "I might have looked like a maniac. A big black man in his twenties with a mane of matted and kinky hair" (17). During the day, he writes in his homemade book "while standing on street corners or sitting on the sidewalk" (17). Then, "at night I'd curl up into a ball in my small corner and dream about my mother (her white skin somehow denying the love she claimed) and my father—his absence even blacker than me" (18). Writing the Bay Area's cultural history offers him no solace because there is still no place for him in this history. Charles E. Wilson Jr. explains that "society makes [Chance] painfully aware of his existence while at the same time, and paradoxically, insisting that he does not actually exist after all. Like Ralph Ellison's famous unnamed protagonist, Chance exists, but only in a state of invisibility."[5] While this new culture of love does not outright reject Chance, it still does not offer him a space in which he can fully know and embrace his racial identity.

When he does finally receive psychiatric treatment after his failed suicide attempt, he claims that the doctors do not understand him because they have not shared his alienating, racialized experiences: "they came from places where they were recognized as members and relatives and citizens. They were never stopped on their front lawn and arrested for stealing their own bicycles the way I had been" (18). Chance then points to race in general, and his mixed-race parentage, as the central factor in his isolation: "I spoke the white man's language. I dreamed his dreams. But when I woke up, no one recognized me. No one but my mother, and I hated her for that" (18). Chance cannot escape race-based self-hatred because he realizes that even the language he uses to try to tell his story is the language of the world that does not "see" him as part of its story.

Chance and his struggles are not, however, invisible to Ordé and the mysterious force behind the blue light. Ordé tells Chance, in fact, that his alienation was why he "was open to the promise of blue light. My life was free from the identity *half-life* had made for itself. I was ready, the Prophet said, to go further than man and his pathetic telos" (18). Chance's experience with racism and alienation makes him "more receptive to the unorthodox knowledge consistent with blue light,"[6] and among the Blues, "African American consciousness is no longer a marginal concept but a visibly central one and one in which African American identity can be experienced in multifarious ways."[7] So, when Chance decides to write his *History* about the blue light instead of about Bay Area counterculture, he realizes his dream of being written into history in general and his own history in particular. He reports that "now it came to me and I was a piece of that history. Like my hero Thucydides, I was part of some of the most important events in the history of the world" (83).

Chance's ability to write this inclusive story, though, depends on his ability to access knowledge about the events that shape it. This knowledge comes to him primarily through the highly metaphorical blood ritual, in which Ordé mixes blood into a powerful "potion" that allows the drinker to see events from the blood contributors' pasts. When Ordé mixes his "lighter" white blood with Chance's "darker" black blood, the mixture first congeals into "fat worms" that then settle into an "almost white" or "milky pink" liquid. Ordé is happy with this whiteness because the followers who "drank a darker fluid" had died (47).

After ingesting the mixture, Chance describes seeing a text: "A pane of light opened before me. It shone like a parchment burning with alien inscriptions, equations, and hieroglyphics. I stared at the burning pages as they moved past" (48). Most of the text is mysterious; it provides "precious little knowledge" (48). But part of this text "was the full biography of Ordé. His childhood as a liar and his adult life as a saint. I saw and felt everything he had known and done up until the moment of blue light," and then "there was a flash and then I was, myself, a page. [. . .] A blank sheet. [. . .] An unwritten footnote" (48). Racial amalgamation/reconciliation—signified by the blood mixing—gives Chance the vision and motivation as well as some, but not all, of the knowledge he needs for his personal and cultural narrative.

The whiteness of the blood potion suggests, though, that the blue light and its followers are not immune from the potentially alienating effects of social stratification and privilege. Half lights, for example, "can never ascend" and "only have the slight possibility of half knowledge." Ordé tells Chance, "You may perceive that there is truth beyond you, but you will never know it, you will never glide between the stars on webs of unity" (44). Chance equates the Blues with "a pantheon of gods," who "heralded an evolution that would become the divinity their mortal lower halves had always dreamed of" (32). By the end of the novel, though, the half lights have become the workers in Treaty, while the Blues are quasi-despotic, and "they rarely laughed or played" (245). Chance first posits "that they had become in some way the Platonic ideals," but then he decides that "these ideals, being beyond human idealism, had turned in on themselves, and so you had the philosopher without humanity, the lover who felt no love" (245). In their self-proclaimed quest to save *all* of humanity, the Blues lose all remnants of their *own* humanity.

Chance's traumatic racialized history and his previous experience with "invisibility" make him uniquely capable of recognizing these corrosive social stratifications that begin to emerge among the Blues and half lights and then among the half lights themselves (268). Winch Fargo, for example, calls Chance "Big Nigger with the Woodbook" (269). As he watches the Blues' meeting about the Gray Man, he does not understand any of the plans because "the music was too powerful for my halfwit senses" (283). Chance has his first "real friendships" in Treaty, though, so he feels connected to the Blues and their community, despite their growing differences (267). In contrast, when the Gray Man chooses to ignore Chance on his way to Treaty, Chance resolves, "he felt that I was beneath his notice. I was intent on making that his big mistake" (286).

At the narrative's close, Chance reveals that he has been recounting the entire story from his book. The acts of reading and writing in general—and the acts of reading and writing *history* specifically—become Chance's key to understanding the mystery of his story and the story of the Blues. The novel complicates this resolution, though, by questioning Chance's narrative integrity. Although Chance's ability to reflect on his diagnoses suggests a mental clarity that is uncharacteristic of his supposed conditions, he is nevertheless institutionalized and drugged. He "suffers" from "second sight"—reminiscent of W. E. B. DuBois's theory of double-consciousness—which, he explains, "makes everything I see different no matter how many times I see it. I could see a tree a thousand times, and in every encounter, the tree would have something new to say to me" (246). In the psychiatric hospital, though, he is "learning how not to use my second sight. All the drugs they give me help dampen the visions" (295–96).

Still, he says, "At least they let me keep my history. When I sit down and read the words, I know that it all must have happened. No one could make up all of that" (295). In this quintessentially postmodern metanarrative twist, the authorial voice of the novel challenges Chance's truth-is-stranger-than-fiction-based argument for his *History*'s—and thus his own memory's—veracity. Someone *could* make it all up: Walter Mosley. Chance himself actually foreshadowed this objection (and responded to it) earlier in the text. About the origins of the material in his *History*, he explains, "It doesn't really matter how I learned what I know, not now anyway. Maybe in some far-flung future, when science is not estranged from the soul, someone may find this text and know how to believe in it" (102).

Diablerie

Diablerie opens with Ben Dibbuk looking at his daughter Seela's new apartment in the East Village, thinking about his general lack of emotion or sentiment, and describing his ongoing affair with Svetlana, a twenty-one-year-old Russian graduate student. Ben maintains a generally strained and asexual, yet nevertheless committed, relationship with his wife, Mona, a freelance editor. Mona cons Ben into attending a reception to celebrate the launch of a new magazine, *Diablerie*. At the event, Barbara "Star" Knowland approaches Ben and tries to talk to him about their time together in Colorado. Star is enraged and suspicious when he claims not to recognize her, but Ben tries to explain that he remembers little from the years when he lived in Colorado and was constantly intoxicated. After this encounter with Star, Ben's relationship with Mona begins to deteriorate further, his enigmatic dreams return, and his disillusionment intensifies. Ben discovers that Mona is having an affair with her coworker, Harvard Rollins (who Ben calls "Harvard Yard") and that the lovers are investigating Ben's past and his connections to Barbara.

Ben then starts feeling more and more erratic and out of control of his life. He is troubled by his violent urges, blackouts, and seemingly random recollections of his drunken past in Colorado. He starts trying to piece together what happened with Barbara more than twenty years earlier. As he does so, he realizes that his life for the past two decades has been boring and redundant, and he decides to leave Mona. When Ben finds out that Mona and Harvard Rollins are not only investigating him, but are also planning to run a story on him and his past in *Diablerie*, he turns to his only friend, Cassius "Cass" Copland, for help. Cass—the security chief for Ben's employer, Our Bank—first offers to kill Barbara, but Ben refuses.

Ben is then approached by Winston Meeks from the Colorado District Attorney's Office. Meeks tells Ben about the murder, nearly twenty-five years earlier, of Sean Messier, and reveals that Barbara has now officially accused Ben of the crime. When Ben confronts Barbara, she recounts the story of the night in June 1979 that she and Ben plotted to steal a trunk and some cash from Sean, Barbara's boyfriend at the time. When he caught Ben and Barbara having sex in his living room, however, Sean and Ben went outside to fight. Ben returned alone and left abruptly; Barbara went outside to look for Sean and found him dead, his skull crushed. Barbara then fled to Berkeley in Sean's car.

Even upon hearing Barbara's story, Ben still does not remember his role, if any, in the killing, and he begins to suspect that it was actually Barbara who killed Sean and is now trying to frame him because she was recently acquitted of other murders. Nevertheless, Ben is arrested. He begins to fear that he will spend the rest of his life in prison, but an FBI agent, sent by Cass, comes to release him. Ben then hides out in a hotel room. Meanwhile, *Diablerie* releases a new issue, featuring a brief story on the murder and Ben's potential involvement. Cass gets a high-powered attorney for Ben, who agrees to be interviewed and take a polygraph test for Winston Meeks. The police finally decide not to prosecute Ben, and instead charge Barbara with the crime. Ben moves in with Svetlana, who is pregnant, and one night, Ben, through a dream, remembers killing Sean in self-defense.

Ben's life story, like Chance's, is incomplete, fragmented, and ultimately still mysterious even at the novel's end. Ben seems to remember killing Sean Messier, but this memory is nevertheless from a dream that has been undoubtedly shaped by temporal distance, trauma, and the facts gleaned from/suggested by Barbara Knowland's version of the narrative. Both Ben's initial repression of the memory of the events surrounding Sean's death and his reconstruction of those events twenty years later can be linked to his desire to find control over his life, and he needs this control as a way to cope with a past defined by violence that stems from racial oppression. Ben denies that race is a factor in his life, but the psychological divisions he creates are linked to his father's social struggles and his own traumatic experience with racialized violence. His ultimate reconstruction of the details of the Messier killing liberates him, then, because it demonstrates his ability to fight back against not only radicalized violence but also the emotional trauma that violence creates.

Before he understands this trauma and its source, though, Ben finds the control he seeks both in a disconnected, mundane life and, most importantly, through "the void." Ben uses his lost interest in reading as a metaphor for this lack of feeling or interest in his world and the people in it. Although he once read often, he "had given up that habit somewhere along the way; lost interest in that narrative line" because, while "everything in a novel leads somewhere" for Ben, "that's not the way life works"; rather, it is "infinitely tedious or depraved" (31).[8] He explains, "I wrote down hexadecimal computer code, day in and day out. Mona flitted from one silly magazine to another. There was no plot, no resolution, revelation, character development—or even any change other than the fact that we got older" (31). He has, according to Owen E. Brady and Derek C. Maus, "constructed" a "benumbed and deceitful life for himself."[9] On these grounds, *New York Times* reviewer Renee Graham connects Ben Dibbuk to the Jewish "dybbuk," who "is a living person possessed by the malevolent spirit of the dead."[10]

To cope with the tedium and depravity, Ben creates "a void." Ben has what he describes as "the feeling that lurked in my shoulder blades[. . . .] Not an emotion or something physical like pain or heat or cold, it was more akin to a void, a sensual numbness" (2). He clarifies: "it wasn't that I felt nothing—not exactly," but he does not feel the expected or even the appropriate emotion (2). When looking at his daughter's new substandard apartment, for instance, he "couldn't feel for her safety"; instead he "couldn't feel anything but dread of the roaches teeming, unseen but still there" (2).

This void, or "lack of sentiment," does not really bother Ben "unless Mona or Seela would complain," and he does not try to even understand or address it until the *Diablerie* party when he meets Barbara. The magazine launch is a fitting context for this meeting because *Diablerie*'s "stories are about the world today, about how to get ahead and stay there without going mad. It also covers some of the stories about people who were given up for lost but who made it back by resuscitating themselves when the monitor had gone flatline" (23). "One of those women," the banquet's emcee explains, "is Barbara Knowland" (23). Barbara, whose name, "Know-land," indicates that she, as Ben suggests, "knew something about me that I myself did not know" (67), also brings Ben back to life by reconnecting him with the repressed narratives of his past.

Ben's transformation begins almost immediately after the party and manifests first in an uncharacteristically passionate sexual encounter with Mona. Confronting Ben about his overly aggressive lovemaking, Mona says, "You didn't see that look in your eye. It was like, like you hated me." Ben replies, "I don't hate anybody," and thinks to himself, "*nor do I love or fear or worry about anyone*" (31, emphasis in original). He later reflects on the incident: "The idea of me, Ben Dibbuk, losing control, even for a moment, was ridiculous. [. . .] There was no unrestrained side to me. It was just sex. Good sex. Nasty, low-down, hard-fucking sex. That's not losing control. That's just human" (32). At this beginning stage in his transformation, Ben does not realize the connection between his emotional and sexual awakening. His sudden interest in the physical elements of "human" instinct suggests that Barbara's story has ignited a raw, senseless passion in Ben—the kind of passion that also leads to murder.

As the novel unfolds, Ben's sexual encounters with his mistress, Svetlana (Lana), also become a key vehicle for helping Ben understand his past and reconstruct the missing narrative of Sean Messier's death. The changes in Ben's relationship with Lana in general, and in their sexual relationship specifically, are a lens that magnifies his underlying emotional changes. Even early in their relationship, Ben realizes that Lana is "emotopathic," in that "she could read the feelings rolling off almost anyone and say the things that they needed to hear" (39). When Ben asks her about a previous sexual encounter in which he blacked out and violently dropped her, she says she liked it and later masturbated at the memory of it: "I was simultaneously aroused and petrified. Svetlana's almost masculine admission, her leaning there on top of me, reminded me of something that, at the same time, I could not remember. It was naked desire with none of the little modesty and lies that I was used to" (41). She also notices the change in him and embraces it. She even tells him that, while she had previously seen their relationship as casual or just physical, she is now falling in love with him because, she explains, "you are like a new boyfriend to me. Dark and filled with secrets, smoking at my table and crying in my bed. You are a new man for me, a second secret lover who throws me down on the floor and takes me" (69).

Lana's observations lead Ben to see these changes himself. He reports, "it occurred to me that Lana was right. I was a much different man than I had been just a day before" (70). Throughout Ben's transformation, he continues to detail their intense sexual encounters and Lana's increased interest in both him and his sex. In so doing, he shows how discovering what Reginald Martin terms "the erotic self" leads to clearer self-knowledge in general. In his introduction to *Black Eros,* Martin explains, "the erotic self must be known to the bearer of its mark or all other aspects of the self's psychic circle suffer from too much or too little attention; the psyche searches for its truest self, and only once the truest self is found can the psyche turn to developing the other parts of the self that remain unknown."[11] This self-knowledge is so integral to Ben's journey in the novel that, by the end of the text, he claims that it is Lana who has "shown me the way" to a redemptive understanding of both love and pain.

Another key figure in Ben's development is his therapist, Dr. Shriver, who leads Ben to a clearer understanding of his father and therefore the original source of the "void." The novel shows the intricate connection between Lana, Shriver's sessions, and the father by combining all three in a kind of narrative free-association. Lana tells Ben, "I don't care [. . .] if you have killed some-body. It's all right with me. You are a good man. You are good to me. I love you." (109) Then the narrative immediately shifts to the doctor's office again and describes how Ben has come to be afraid of the doctor's couch and the memories he has conjured up there. When Ben lies back and closes his eyes, Dr. Shriver says, "Tell me about your father," and Ben reports, "a rush of calm went through my fearful mind [. . .]" (109). Detailed memories of his father, including his father's "big black hands" that beat him, closely follow (109).

This brief mention of the father's skin color is one of the few racial markers in the text, and the epiphanies Ben has through his time with Dr. Schriver are also linked to race through the African artifacts in the therapist's office. The doctor is a "rangy white man," but his office decor is "African images: masks, paintings, photographs, and jewelry" (93). Ben remembers, "When I had first come to his office, he tried to engage me about African culture. [. . .] But he

soon realized that I knew nothing about that continent, that dark unconsciousness of the hundred million displaced descendants of slaves. I didn't know and I
didn't want to know" (93). Although Ben rejects cultural connections to Africa,
the feelings of displacement and "dark unconsciousness" that he associates
with "that continent" parallel his descriptions of his own emotions throughout
the text and speak to possible motivation for his father's violence.

Beaten down by a system that hated and devalued him, Ben's father, in turn,
beat his children for even the most minor infractions. Ben reports that, after an
emotional conversation with his mother, "My father, who loved me as much as
nuns love God, had to beat me in order to stave off the demons that bedeviled
him" (147), and he later adds: "My father beat me and I loved him for it. Not in
spite of the pain but because he touched me with care, no matter how violently.
He needed me to crawl and so I crawled. He needed me to hide from the light of
others' feelings and so I built myself a shell out of alcohol and then later with
that feeling in my shoulders[. . . .] It didn't matter. I had loved him from the
first moment we met. I would keep on loving him until breath left me" (168).

Ben's healing from the wounds of his father's violence comes when he
decides to see the violence as a misguided manifestation of love. He sees his father's beatings as a feeble attempt at connection from a man who—because of
his own emotional inadequacies likely fueled by years as a victim of systematic
racism—knew no other way to forge those connections.

The novel's other significant nod to race's role in Ben's life and recovery
comes when Ben attends a talk that he had seen advertised in the newspaper.
The talk features "a lawyer who specialized in death row cases. [. . .] He talked
about the number of people and people of color in prison. He spoke about
how the law was anything but equal and fair" (101). Ben's initial response is,
"I didn't care about any of that either. I had been a black man in America for
five decades, almost, and nothing about that meant anything to me. Life for
all Americans, whether they knew it or not, was like playing blackjack against
the house—sooner or later you were going to lose" (101). However, he has no
doubt that, if he were put on trial for killing Sean, he would be convicted and
sent to prison for the rest of his life. Although Ben is unwilling or unable to
admit race's role in this certainty, Barbara Knowland's wrongful conviction at
the end of the novel underscores the reality of the racially biased system. Ben
cannot save her because the only "proof" he has of his own innocence is his
dreams.

Like *Blue Light*, *Diablerie* leaves the veracity of its central narrative in
question, but just as Chance finds emotional solace in the simple reading of his
History, Ben finds solace in these dreamy memories of Sean Messier's killing.

"Amnesia," reviewer Elisabeth Vincentelli asserts, is one of the great tropes of genre fiction because it involves people (re)discovering themselves and their capabilities."[12] Regardless of whether the narrative is true, Ben now believes it is true. He knows that he can stand up to racialized violence, and he has escaped an unjust "justice" system.

CHAPTER SIX

Hero or Villain?
Philosophical Fictions

Although most of Walter Mosley's characters walk fine moral lines, his mysteries and other genre fictions give their characters these moral quandaries in service of a primary narrative. In what might be termed Mosley's "philosophical" fictions, however, these moral questions become key narrative conflicts. These non-genre-focused works include the short-story collections *Always Outnumbered, Always Outgunned* (1998, starring the fan-favorite Socrates Fortlow) and *The Tempest Tales* (2008, starring the irreverent Tempest Landry, an homage to Langston Hughes's Jesse B. Semple), as well as the critically acclaimed novel *The Man in My Basement* (2004) and the critically ignored novel *The Last Days of Ptolemy Grey* (2010). In each of these texts, the main characters find themselves in an almost epic battle to not only recognize the difference between good and evil in both themselves and others, but also to choose the course of action that best serves a greater good, even when that action conflicts with the dominant morality that the text's world espouses.

Always Outnumbered, Always Outgunned

Mosley writes in *Twelve Steps Toward Political Revelation* (2011), "Socrates realized that he was the smartest man in Athens because he knew his deficiencies and limitations, his ignorance."[1] Like his namesake, convicted murderer and rapist Socrates Fortlow's genius comes from the stunning clarity of his self-awareness. In *Always Outnumbered, Always Outgunned,* he struggles to control his rage, which at times borders on bloodlust, but he is also dedicated to making amends for his past in general and his violent crimes in particular. In this struggle, because of Socrates's intimate knowledge of evil—a knowledge he acquired from learning to understand the innate evil in himself—he is often more capable of seeing innate "goodness," or value, in actions or individuals that the world around him might otherwise dismiss or misjudge. He also demonstrates the value of penance through his commitment to self-judgment and moral balance.

All of the stories in *Always Outnumbered, Always Outgunned* speak to these themes, but they are especially evident in the collection's most prominent recurring thread—Socrates's mentoring of the troubled youth Darryl. In the first story, "Crimson Shadow," Socrates catches Darryl after he has just killed Socrates's pet rooster, Billy. Enraged, Socrates pulls Darryl into his house and makes Darryl help him prepare a meal out of the slain bird. Darryl becomes more comfortable with Socrates as they cook and eat together, and Darryl eventually reveals that he killed a young boy that he and his friends were bullying. Socrates tells Darryl that he needs to do some kind of penance to make up for his crime, and he adds that Darryl is welcome to visit anytime.

Darryl takes Socrates up on his offer and comes back to see Socrates in the story "Marvane Street." Socrates once again prepares a meal for Darryl, and the two discuss dreams and nightmares. Darryl describes the nightmare he has every night in which the boy he killed chases him through a dark room, and Darryl asks for Socrates's help to make the dreams stop. Darryl sleeps at Socrates's apartment while the older man plans a "lesson" for Darryl. As part of this lesson, Socrates takes Darryl to Marvane Street, where they pass a drug house, the headquarters of a group called the Young Africans, and a nondescript building across from a woman named Luvia's boarding house. Socrates points out that the police are using the latter building to spy on the Young Africans while ignoring the drug house. Socrates explains that Luvia, who selflessly cares for her needy boarders and neighbors, is the only honorable person on Marvane Street. Darryl tells Socrates that he is worried about gangs or other kids trying to harm or kill him, and Socrates promises to protect him.

In "Lessons," Socrates does so. The story begins after Darryl has been living with Socrates for a few months. Socrates is recounting a dream he has about his mother while the pair wait for Darryl's nemesis, Philip, and his gang. When the boys arrive, Socrates steps away with a friend to allow Darryl space to confront the boys on his own. The boys start fighting, however, and Darryl is quickly overwhelmed. Socrates intervenes, knocking down and disarming the boys. After the fight, Socrates realizes that Darryl can no longer stay with him because the boys will eventually find them. Luvia reluctantly agrees to ask Hallie and Costas McDaniels, who had recently lost their own son in a shootout, to take Darryl. They agree, and Darryl leaves tearfully.

Socrates is drawn to Darryl because he sees that the younger man could become a hardened criminal like Socrates. Socrates understand the social and familial factors that led him to become a killer and sees that Darryl still has the potential to rise above them. Socrates has "a recognition of his younger self in Darryl,"[2] so mentoring Darryl becomes a way for Socrates to both pay penance for his own sins and save Darryl.

In order to realize both of these goals, Socrates must teach Darryl self-judgment and practice it himself. When he catches Darryl killing Billy the rooster and tries to confront him about the crime, Socrates reassures his young captive, "I ain't your warden, li'l brother. I ain't gonna show you to no jail. I'm just talkin' to ya—one black man to another one. If you don't hear me there ain't nuthin' I could do" (22).[3] He recognizes Darryl's fear and anxiety, but Socrates also realizes that he must actively try to reach out to Darryl, even if the task appears pointless.

After Darryl confesses to murdering the boy in the park, Socrates encourages him to look beyond the evil of the action and beyond the guilt that accompanies that action to instead focus on being honest with himself about who he is and who he wants to be. Socrates explains, "I'm sayin' that I think you was wrong for killin' that boy. I know you killed 'im. I know that you couldn't help it. But you was wrong anyway. An' if that's the truth, an' if you could say it, then maybe you'll learn sumpin'. Maybe you'll laugh in the morning sometimes again" (22). Healing can only come through honest self-awareness and evaluation, through balancing knowledge of the evil of the past with hope for the potential of the future: "'We all got to be our own judge, li'l brother,' Socrates elaborates, ''Cause if you don't know when you wrong then yo' life ain't worf a damn'" (22).

Socrates struggles with his own inner demons, though, as he guides Darryl through these lessons. Watching Darryl eat, "Socrates wanted to stifle the rages that bloomed in his chest. He wanted to slap the skinny boy out of his chair, to see him sprawled out on the floor. He wanted to pick Darryl up by those bony shoulders and slam him up against the wall[. . . .] He wished some man had had that kind of love for him before he'd gone wrong" (80). During the meal, Darryl "seemed angry," and while eating makes his anger subside somewhat, "Socrates was mad too. He could see that Darryl was in trouble. And trouble was always close to violence in Socrates' life" (81). Socrates's rage is powerful, but he is able to recognize it and balance the negative energy with the positive energy he puts into his own penance, helping Darryl.

He then teaches Darryl to do the same. He instructs: "As long as you alive you could do somethin'. That's what bein' alive is all about. When you dead then your doin' days is over. It's over for that boy. He's dead. He's dead and you killed him an' now you feel bad. So you got to do sumpin'. An' since you did wrong now you got to do a good thing. Try an' balance it out" (82). The "good thing" to "balance it out" cannot, Socrates understands, be just any good deed; it needs to be a foil or direct response to the original transgression. Socrates therefore tells Darryl, "'Fore you could do sumpin' you gotta know what the problem is," and when Darryl articulates his fear of being killed by a gang, Socrates tells him, "That's yo' problem right there, Darryl[. . . .] To try'n think of a way that children don't get killed. Try'n make it better for whoever you can" (85).

Ironically, we don't see Darryl fulfill this change in any of this stories in this volume. Socrates, however, does: he figures out a way for Darryl not to be killed and stops Darryl from killing Philip and his gang. In his critique of the Young Africans, Socrates says, "You don't teach people, you love 'em. You don't get a house and a printin' press and put up a fence. You do like Luvia. You open up your arms and your pocketbook" (91). Socrates saves Darryl initially through physical intervention, but ultimately by loving him—and by opening up his arms and pocketbook to secure him a safer home with Hallie and Costas.

Socrates's dreams affirm his direction with Darryl. Just as Darryl is able to squelch his night terrors with the simple thought of making amends for his sins, Socrates earns a dreamed reconnection with his mother by saving Darryl. After he takes Darryl to Marvane Street, Socrates dreams about a place called "Souls End," which is "the graveyard for all the black people that had died from grief" (94). There, a large, "jet-black man" tells Socrates to dig up all the graves, and when Socrates protests that he "cain't do it," the man simply replies "But you could try!" (94).

The gravedigger suggests that Socrates needs to persevere with Darryl, even though the results seem at best uncertain and at worst impossible. This sentiment echoes the volume's title, which comes from an exchange between Socrates and Darryl after the altercation with Philip. Socrates praises Darryl: "You stood up for yourself, Darryl[. . . .] That's all a black man could do. You always outnumbered, you always outgunned" (131). As critic Charles Wilson argues, "If one is 'always outnumbered' and 'always outgunned,' then one confronts a life fraught with unfairness, injustice, and general confusion. In short, the novel's overarching theme is the extraordinary difficulty of ordinary life. This reality is reinforced by the fact that everyone must, however, strive to endure. Even when faced with social, political, or economic oppression, one must militate against all obstacles to sustain a life that, by its very inception, is meant to thrive." [4]

Darryl, confused by the reflection, replies, "But they gonna still be after me[. . . .] They still gonna wanna get me," to which Socrates counters, "That's right [. . . .] But now you done stood up. Now you done your best, so you don't have nutin' to be sorry for—not ever again in your life" (131). Both Socrates and the dream man understand that victory is often unlikely, but it is the struggle for that victory—the struggle to do what is right even when it is impossible—that defines a man's value.

Giving up Darryl to Hallie and Costas is another great struggle for Socrates, but it is his last option for saving Darryl. When Darryl suggests that he would be able to protect himself if he were more like Socrates, the ex-con replies, "No, Darryl, you don't want to be like me. [. . .] You don't want run wild in the street treatin' women like they was dogs. Fightin' and' stealin' and actin' up till they put you in jail. Naw, man, you wanna get out from under all that shit" (132). Darryl then says, "But I'ont know how," and Socrates does not respond (132). This silence suggests that Socrates also does not know how, so he must turn Darryl's care over to the Christians, Hallie and Costas. Socrates "didn't like Hallie and Costas. They were cowed and cowardly, he thought. But he also loved them because they had the power to do what he could not" (137).

Socrates's dreams again affirm his decisions—this time by granting him the mother-love he has so desperately missed since his incarceration. At the beginning of the story "The Lesson," as he sits with Darryl in the park before the fight, he recounts seeing his mother in a dream, but she says nothing; after the fight, in the middle of this story, she begins to take a step toward him; and by the end, after Socrates gives up Darryl, she walks over and embraces him, bringing the "best sleep that he could remember" (139).

The Tempest Tales

The Tempest Tales—a series of stories "Dedicated to the Memory of Langton Hughes" and written in the style of Hughes's "Simple Tales" from the 1940s and 1950s—follows folk hero Tempest Landry after he is shot by police and sent to St. Peter for judgment in the afterlife. As the angel reads the list of Tempest's sins, Tempest has a justification for each one. Patient at first, Peter eventually tires of Tempest's insolence and tells him to "Go to hell!" (14).[5] Tempest not only refuses to go, but refuses to even accept that he is damned, at least without acceptable explanation, for the sins Peter listed.

Tempest then wakes up back in Harlem three years later with a new face and a personal "accounting Angel," Joshua, who is also the collection's narrator. Joshua tells Tempest that he has been sent back to earth "to reexamine" his life until he is ready to accept Peter's judgment and that if he does not accept this judgment, "there will be a great turmoil in the heavens" (15).

The stories that follow chronicle Joshua's attempts to convince Tempest that he is a sinner and Tempest's continued resistance to that verdict. The pair engage in a series of debates about topics such as fate, justice, empathy, sin, and experience. The collection is divided into nearly equal parts: "The Fall"—which focuses narrowly on Tempest's conflicts with Joshua and his "accounting" principles—and "The Apple"—which adds the devil into the conflict and conversations. Each story within these sections has a unique moral focus, but taken together, they suggests that Tempest—based in part on his experience as a black man in American—has more insight into human morality than either the "accounting angel," Joshua, who judges him, or the devil, who seeks to use Tempest's logical defiance to destroy heaven. Tempest's rational, yet experiential, approach to life and morality threatens the rules and absolutes that are the foundation for both heaven and hell, and Tempest's questions and reflections eventually offer two alternatives to Joshua's absolutist model: grace and sacrifice.

Tempest immediately challenges Joshua's dichotomous understanding of right and wrong, and he suggests that race must play a role in that understanding. In "Charity," Tempest explains his rationale for stealing money from a contribution box in order to get settled after St. Peter put him back in New York with no money, no job, and no apartment. He also questions how his God will judge the circumstances of his death. When Joshua claims the cops shooting Tempest was "accidental," Tempest replies, "You don't take no scared white boys can't tell the difference between one black man and another, give 'em guns, and let 'em run around the streets of Harlem and then say it was an accident when they one day shoot down an innocent man" (18). Similarly, in the chapter "Kingdom of Heaven," Tempest complicates Joshua's ideas about free will, arguing that racism affects choice. Joshua suggests that "there is no race in heaven," and Tempest counters, "We ain't in heaven, brother. This is New York City. This is where I washed up though no fault of my own. Down here the color of your skin means somethin'" (26). Tempest's arguments recall Harriet Jacobs's insistence that, because she is subjected to unspeakable violence and oppression, "the slave woman ought not to be judged by the same standard as others."[6]

By the third chapter, "Desire," Joshua has come to fear Tempest's "power to refute the claims of heaven" and the potentially eternal consequences of that power (28). In addition to claiming that heaven's judgments are unfairly ignoring race's role in his actions, Tempest charges that an angel cannot judge him because angels have never known human passion or suffering. Joshua admits that he "studied passion" but has no direct knowledge of human experience (33). So Joshua agrees to let Tempest help him have these experiences.

The experiences, which center on loss and love, eventually show Joshua the limits of heaven's perspective and therefore undermine heaven's authority. Tempest first takes Joshua to meet LaVon Singleton, a dying devout street minster, and in "Trinity" the three men discuss how to earn a place in heaven before LaVon dies at the end of the story. This interaction not only allows Joshua to experience a human's last moment on earth, but it also shows him that Tempest is "clever, even calculating. A man of such intelligence was a greater threat than I had feared" (36).

Then, in "Lady," Joshua encounters Branwyn Meeks, sent by Tempest to confuse the angel. Branwyn tells Joshua how Tempest saved her life, and then the angel and the woman go on Joshua's first date, which ends in his first kiss. Through Branwyn's story, Joshua explains, "It came clear to me then why Tempest angered me so. He was presenting me with a problem where sin existed but there was no simple identification of the sinner" (52). Tempest admits that he sent Branwyn because "I thought she might make you see that when you live in the sin of this world you got to work that sin to try and do good" (55). Similarly, at funeral services for Tempest's aunt in "The Wake," Tempest asserts that the good woman's life showed that "To cure evil [. . .] you gotta live with it. You gotta breathe it and eat it. You gotta call it brother, sleep by its side" (58). The angel is so moved by the stories of the woman's life that he sheds his first tears over a mortal's death.

This unexpected emotion intensifies Joshua's feelings for Branwyn, and in "A New Morning" Joshua succumbs to these feelings and decides to visit his crush. He is devastated to find Tempest there and surprised at his own rage. He recalls, "An angel's sorrow is only evoked, it is said, in sadness at the state of the human race. I cried that night over my own pain. The evil trickster Tempest had finally defeated me by turning my own heart against the logic of heaven" (63). Tempest's culminating emphasis on experience has successfully undermined Joshua's faith in his purely rational model of judgment.

This rejection intensifies when Branwyn chooses Joshua over Tempest in the section's final chapter, "Eternal Love." During his passionate days with his lover, Joshua admits, "Every now and then I even forgot that I was an angel. I didn't care about Tempest or Peter or the fate of the world. All that mattered was her lips saying my name" (82). The jilted Tempest moves to Atlanta, and Joshua admits that, although he remembers that his first responsibility is to save heaven, he is glad to have the extra time on earth to spend loving Branwyn.

The second half of the collection, "The Apple," opens with Joshua and Branwyn caring for their three-month-old baby, Tethamalanianti. In the chapter "Fear and Dread," Joshua has found such a connection with his mortal companions that he says, "it felt like sin it was so powerful, but I knew that it was love" (91). Joshua experiences "fear and dread" when Tempest returns to New York with his "lawyer," Basel Bob—the devil "in the guise of white youth"— who will assist him in arguing his case against heaven (97). Joshua not only feels the weight of the impending contest, but also feels that heaven has abandoned him. He narrates: "this, I knew, was the beginning of the debate between heaven and hell. Every night for the past eight days I sat up late praying for guidance from my celestial masters, but no council came. Here I was, engaged in the most important conflict ever to arise between good and evil—and I was alone, without an ally" (97).

Satan's whiteness, Heaven's abandonment, and Joshua's use of the term "masters" to describe the heavenly power structure create an unlikely alliance between Joshua and Tempest. Although they still disagree on Tempest's fundamental nature and Joshua remains committed to his dualistic perspective on sin and judgment, they are united in their understanding of human suffering and, eventually—when Bob begins to threaten Tempest in "The Door"—in their desire to thwart the devil's designs. Tempest remains, however, committed to his individual salvation—despite both Joshua's and the devil's continued attempts to damn him to hell. As Bob and Joshua debate in "The Ascendance of Man," for example, Tempest joins the conversation with questions that puzzle and worry both men, and he later observes, "I am a black man. I ain't on nobody's side but my own. devil [sic] in Whiteface on one side, heaven and blackface on the other—just make me all the more alone" (113).

Tempest's cosmic solitude—along with heaven's impotence to address it—is especially evident in "The Door," during which the devil shows Tempest a mysterious door—the door to hell—and tells him that, if he does not open it and liberate all of hell's souls to conquer heaven, he will suffer forever under the devil's wrath. This story not only shows Tempest experiencing fear, but also shows Joshua's inability to comfort Tempest while he is distressed. Joshua laments, "For aeons I lived in heaven calculating the wages of sin. But in all that time, sifting through in immeasurable pain, I never once experienced what it was like to be human and to truly know pain. But here I was tutored in what suffering meant by a recalcitrant sinner. Tempest's pain touched me, it pressed in from all sides" (120). Joshua's reflections here evoke the bible itself, specifically Romans 6:23: "For the wages of sin is death, but the gift of God is eternal life through Jesus Christ our Lord." This connection suggests that Joshua is so focused on sin and penance that he has neglected to consider the possibility of grace and forgiveness.

The text emphasizes the possibility of grace again in the following chapter, "Siren." As Joshua sings to his daughter, "Time stopped for a moment. It was a feeling akin to my aeons in heaven. We were full and whole, neither going forward in time nor rehashing the successes and mistakes of the past. It was a moment of *grace*" (122, emphasis added). In the same chapter, Tempest himself brings up forgiveness, for himself and for Bob. Tempest asks, "But if I repented could I go to heaven?" Joshua simply responds, "it's too late for that" (133). Tempest also asks, "What if I convinced Bob to repent?" (133). Joshua does not respond directly to this question but thinks to himself: "I felt fear then because I didn't have an answer. Evil never asked for forgiveness—but what if it did? My heavenly Masters had not communicated with me since my first days from the mortal plane. What impact would be wrought on eternity with my rejection, or acceptance, of Bob's repentance?" (133). Here Joshua admits that forgiveness might be a possibility, even for Satan—and thus certainly for Tempest—but fear paralyzes him from pursuing it.

Ever persistent, Tempest asks about the possibility of "peace talks" between heaven and hell. Bob, however, has come to hate Tempest and his savvy resistance to the devil's charms, so the angel and Tempest decide to try to work together against Bob. As they discuss ways to do this in the chapter "The Balance," they find no common ground, and Tempest again raises questions of grace and forgiveness, this time though sacrifice. He asks Joshua, "What if you offered your soul to Bob? [. . .] For him to spare Branwyn and Titi why don't you give him your soul?" (147).

The angel dismisses the notion, and when Tempest immediately comes back with the question, "Is your soul better than mine, Angel?" Joshua has no response. Instead, his mind jumps to his daughter's namesake, the "great Mayan princess that lived over twelve hundred years ago" and who "was a conundrum in the heavenly court because she killed her father in his sleep" when she found out he was plotting to kill her sons; the princess "was sacrificed on a stone altar, her blood running in rivulets to four golden cups that the four sons all drank from. My daughter's namesake gave up her own life to save her killers" (147). Joshua's subconscious link between Tempest's request and the epitome of selfless sacrifice that his innocent daughter embodies again suggests that Joshua's rules for salvation are not as clear or rigid as he represents them to be.

Without a viable way to defeat Bob, who is putting increasing pressure on Tempest, the damned man decides in "The Call" that he needs to flee New York. Joshua is very surprised, therefore, when Tempest resurfaces a few weeks later in the final chapter, "The Crossroad." He gleefully tells the angel how he convinced the devil to go back to hell by telling him of the realization that the power to reject hell's authority was the same as the power to reject heaven's: Tempest could destroy both with free will. So Bob promises to leave Tempest alone as long as Tempest does not exercise his newly realized power.

Joshua congratulates Tempest: "You made a deal with the devil without selling your soul. [. . .] That is another first" (165). Joshua, however, says that heaven will never make a such a deal. Tempest's tales thus become what *Kirkus Reviews* labels an "anti-catechism."[7] Without divine grace, Tempest must rely on human ingenuity to outwit the devil and save himself not with God, but from God.

The Man in My Basement

The Man in My Basement opens with the obviously rich Anniston Bennet knocking on Charles Blakey's door to inquire about renting Charles's basement for a couple of months in the upcoming summer. At first, Charles refuses, but since he's behind on the mortgage and has no other income prospects because he stole from his previous employer, he decides to reconsider Bennet's offer. Bennet returns to discuss the arrangements and explains that he wants the basement for a sixty-five-day "recluse" and will pay Charles nearly fifty thousand dollars for the space and his services.

Charles invites his friend, Ricky, over to help him clean out the basement, which is not only dusty and dirty, but also filled with family heirlooms. Charles wants to throw everything away or burn it, but Ricky suggests Charles try to sell the artifacts through a dealer/anthropologist, Narciss Gully. Narciss tells Charles that the artifacts could be worth up to a hundred thousand dollars, but she also teaches him about the items' history and cultural value.

Charles then isolates himself for over a month before preparing for Bennet's arrival. Delivery men bring materials and Bennet's handwritten instructions on how to create a "cell" in the basement. When Bennet finally arrives, he explains that his object is to imprison himself for his heinous crimes and that Charles will be his "warden." Over the next few weeks, Bennet and Charles engage in a series of conversations and arguments about the nature of sin, good and evil, justice, and penance. These interactions and the control over Bennet transform Charles. Specifically, they make him more assertive and more interested in his history. He also pursues a relationship with Narciss, who convinces him to start a museum for his artifacts, rather than sell them off, and charge admission to make a profit.

After leaving Bennet alone for days in the dark with only bread and condensed milk, Charles convinces Bennet to confess to all of his crimes. Charles records the conversations, and just days before his release, Bennet kills himself. Charles buries him and destroys the cage.

The novel's central conflict is a battle of wits between confessed evildoer Bennet and Charles, the slacker-turned-warden. In her essay "Devil with the Blue Eyes," Francesca Canadé Sautman argues, more specifically, "*The Man in My Basement,* an allegorical novel built on the psychomachia that pits the narrator against the self-jailed Bennet and couched in the stylistic frameworks of both the detective novel and the political thriller, is adumbrated by thinking on the place of human rights in today's brutal world."[8] Blakey quickly becomes an oppressor when given control over his "prisoner," Bennet, who has caged himself as "penance" for decades of "crimes against humanity" (134).[9] Bennet's reflections and confessions, though, lead the formerly aimless Blakey to explore and embrace his own personal and cultural history, allowing him to "see" himself as well as find a role for himself in his world. In so doing, the novel shows the redemptive potential of Bennet's "alternative" morality that privileges history, self-awareness, and personal accountability.

Before Bennet, Charles was disaffected and alone, with no meaningful connections to his friends, family, or community. "The best moments" of his life were those he spent in solitude, "talking to myself or reading about outer space" (13). He acknowledges that his life is "messed up" (45). He is so detached, even from himself, that when his former coworker confronts him about taking money from the bank, he thinks, "suddenly it all came back to me like the plot of a novel I had read so long ago I didn't even remember the name of the book. But it wasn't that long ago and it was my own life that I was remembering" (28). The six weeks he spends in solitude after he agrees to rent the basement to Bennet are "just a small sample of my whole life up until that time—a waste" (104).

He also cares little, if at all, about his family history and has no sense of racial solidarity, but instead almost boasts about his complete disconnection with black history in general and the history of slavery specifically. He explains, "The Blakeys were indentured servants who earned their freedom. The Dodds were free from the beginning. It was even hinted that they, the Dodds, came straight from Africa at the beginning of the eighteenth century. My parents were both very proud that their ancestors were never slaves" (17). Even when Bennet arrives and tells Charles that the cage lock is "an original lock used to hold down a line of slaves in the old slaving ships," Charles admits that, while he "understood that racism doesn't ask for a pedigree" and "knew that many white people didn't like me because of my dark skin," he "didn't feel the pang or tug of identity when slavery was mentioned" (125).

Charles does not even feel a "tug of identity," though, over his personal history. When he cleans out his basement for Bennet, he finds "six boxes of old books (including three diaries from three generations of Blakeys and Dodds), wooden toys, tools that I couldn't even figure out how to hold, and so many piles of old clothes"—too many for him to sort (53). As he watches Narciss sift through the artifacts to determine their value, he realizes that she is "marking out a history that probably would have captured the interest of historians or anthropologists around the nation" (57). For Charles, though, these artifacts are nothing but "a pile of refuse that, if it weren't for her concern, I would have used to make a bonfire in the back" (57).

Like Ben in Mosley's *Diablerie,* Charles feels little concern over this lack of connection or its causes and effects. His relationship with Bennet, however, changes this, and the conversations become, as *New Yorker* critic Ben Greenman asserts, "a kind of self-help seminar" for Charles.[10] As he comes to understand the nature of sin and repentance through his dialogue with the mysterious white man, he begins to see the roots of his aimlessness. He explains, "Before Anniston Bennet had come into my life, I was invisible, moving silently among the people of the Harbor. No one wondered about me, no one questioned me. Even my best friends simply accepted what they saw" (207). Rather than a man, he reflects, "I might as well have been a tree at the end of the block. People saw me well enough to walk around, but that was just about it" (207).

But this "invisibility" is not one-sided. Charles also "treated everything and everyone around me in the same way. I could put a name on them, maybe. But I rarely touched or spoke a meaningful word to a soul. Weeks could go by and not one worthwhile piece of information would pass between me and another human being" (207). At this turning point, though, "everything was different—half different, really," because "what changed was what I saw. It was as if everybody had become like a mirror, and I saw reflections of what they saw instead of what it was they were trying to show me or tell me" (208). Charles decides this is valuable because, "when I saw or heard something I didn't like, I had the chance to alter my behavior" (208).

This description of Charles's invisibility, especially when considered in combination with the novel's title, conjures Ralph Ellison's *Invisible Man* (1952). In Ellison's notes on the novel, he explains that his nameless narrator's "invisibility" "rings from a great formlessness of Negro life wherein all values are in flux, and where those institutions and patterns which mold the white American's personality are missing or not so immediate in their effect." Essentially, the ambiguity and conflict that are the eminent results of racism lead to the emergence of "personalities of extreme complexity."[11]

These "extreme complexities" alongside the "reflections" Charles describes also evoke W. E. B. DuBois's double-consciousness, a black man's "second sight," which "only lets him see himself through the revelation of the other world" and leads to a "sense of always looking at one's self through the eyes of others." For DuBois, "The history of the American Negro" is embodied in the struggle "to attain self-conscious manhood, to merge his double self into a better and truer self."[12] While DuBois also thought that African Americans were "gifted with [this] second sight," Charles's descriptions of his reflected self-perspective is distinctly more hopeful. This tone, however, suggests naïveté since he is only seeing a reflection of himself, which would be (by nature) at best modified or inverted and at worst completely obscured or distorted by the reflective surface, the reflective subject's identity.

Although Charles himself recounts few direct interactions with racism, the artifacts that fill his basement—his home's foundation—have monetary and historical value because of the racialized struggles that they speak to and document. In addition, Bennet's extreme, fabricated whiteness—highlighted by his artificially bald head and blue contacts that cover his entire eye—contrasts starkly with and thus draws attention to Charles's blackness. Because of the crimes he has committed in Africa, Bennet tells Charles, "I need a black face to look in on me. No white man has the right" (174). Later, he elaborates, "I chose you so that Anniston Bennet, the whitest white man that I could think up, would be jailed by a black man who was really a blue blood in American history" (219).

Bennet, ironically, sees Charles and his history more clearly that Charles does himself. Charles appreciates this and agrees to Bennet's incarceration primarily because "he knew more about me that any other person" (124). The novel underscores Bennet's profound connection to Charles's past by linking Bennet to the passport masks that also help push Charles toward greater self-awareness. Narciss explains that the masks "were used as identification but also as a way of bringing home along when you were away on a long journey," and because Charles's family's masks were made from ivory, she posits, "they might have belonged to rich men, maybe even royalty" (96). She insists that Charles keep the masks, rather than include them with the other items to be sold, and he develops an attachment to them. He names them, talks to them, and generally "communes" with them, observing, "I didn't know a damn thing about them except that my family had kept and then forgotten them in the basement for hundreds of years. They were the only thing in my life of value right then— a hope that I came from somewhere important" (196).

Even early in the story, when he first sees the masks, Narciss tells Charles that the masks are "the history of your history." Charles reflects, "the words came to me as truth" (63). Soon after he feels this "truth," Charles remarks that Bennet reminds him of the artifacts because "his head was oval and his chin came to a tip like the masks" (71–72). Such a link reinforces that both the masks and the relationship with Charles lead to a deeper understanding of his history.

This connection between the otherwise nefarious Bennet and the beautiful, richly historical masks also problematizes Bennet's proclamation that he is "the worst demon" and suggests that his rejection of conventional morality may have merit (217). Bennet, for example, claims not to "recognize an organized form of law enforcement, or government for that matter, as valid" because "there is no justice unless the judged agree. Without understanding and repentance there can only be revenge" (120–21). Bennet explains of his self-incarceration, "I am doing so because I am guilty, not because I was caught. And in so doing I am making the world a better place. I'm setting an example down here" (134). This example is necessary, Devika Sharma notes, because it is "Bennet's attempt to subject himself to some sort of moral and social control, since no ordinary juridical arrangements recognize his crimes as crimes."[13] Charles, therefore, realizes that Bennet is "a kind of mastermind, a Moriarty or Iago. A man who had been across the line of lies that defined good and evil for most normal folks" (150). At the same time, Charles also understands that Bennet's perspective on life and morality has liberating value. Bennet, therefore, becomes a kind of "martyr" in that "it was like one of those death-row inmates that they interview just before the sentence is executed. You see the evil they have caused, but you still feel like death is not the answer—that killing this man would in some strange way take away his victim's last hope" (173). The presence and understanding of evil help reveal and define the good—just as Bennet's constructed white identity helps Charles better understand his personal and historical black identity.

A legacy built on an understanding of evil, however, is not without complications: the knowledge and understanding of evil can create a separation from the joyful elements of human existence. In his suicide letter, for example, Bennet writes, "I want to die telling you something, Charles. I want to pass something on, but I can't think of a thing" (246). Having confessed all of his sins to Charles during his last days in the cage, he has no other stories left. Sin—along with redemption for that sin—was his only narrative. Charles, meanwhile, has found purpose in his history and in showcasing that history through his museum. However, he also concludes, "I still haven't found love, and whenever I think about children, I remember that there was once a boy who was sold to a dog"—recalling one of Bennet's more heinous stories (249). Knowing the potential for evil in the world prevents him from opening himself up to anything or anyone that the evil could destroy.

The Last Days of Ptolemy Grey

The Last Days of Ptolemy Grey enacts the temporal confusion of its title character, beginning with an "Afterword," a letter from ninety-one-year-old Ptolemy to seventeen-year-old Robyn Small, the young woman who would become simultaneously his caretaker and his ward. The letter foreshadows Ptolemy's emergence from dementia and his quest to both avenge his grand-nephew Reggie's death and fulfill a life-changing promise made to a childhood friend, Coydog McCann.

At the opening of the narrative proper, Ptolemy is living alone in his dis-
gustingly dirty and messy apartment. Almost completely lost in time and in
his fragmented memories, Ptolemy anticipates a visit from Reggie, who checks
in on him and helps him with shopping and other errands. Ptolemy's great-
grandnephew, Hilly, comes instead, though, because Reggie has been murdered
in a drive-by shooting.

Ptolemy meets Robyn at Reggie's wake, and they are instantly drawn to
each other. Robyn takes Reggie's place as Ptolemy's caretaker: she cleans his
apartment, sorts through his horded piles, and organizes his finances. Robyn
comes to live with Ptolemy as his ward, and he offers to share his substantial
life savings with her. Robyn's aid and attention—and the sense of control that
she creates for Ptolemy—not only lead to more intense flashbacks to his childhood talks and experiences with Coydog, but also inspire him to pursue treatment for his dementia.

Ptolemy's social worker refers him to Dr. Bryant Ruben, who offers an ex-
perimental drug that will give him the clarity he wants but will likely kill him
within weeks. Ptolemy agrees to the treatment over Robyn's objections. The
medicine's initial doses put Ptolemy in a four-day fever dream, and during this
dream he relives his final moments with Coydog. Shortly before he is lynched,
the beloved mentor Coydog tells the boy Ptolemy about the gold coins he stole
from a white slaveholder and about how the "treasure" should be used to help
"poor black folks treated like they do us" (140).[14] Ptolemy also recalls other previously lost formative memories, such as meeting and courting his wife, Sensia,
and her sudden death.

He awakens from the dream, though, with fully renewed clarity and purpose. Although somewhat physically weakened by a persistent fever, Ptolemy
quickly begins the work he wants to accomplish before his death. He makes
Robyn his legal heir and shows her how to cash in the gold so she can continue
to support herself and Reggie's children. He also figures out that Reggie's wife's
lover, Alfred, orchestrated Reggie's murder. When Ptolemy confronts Alfred,
the murderer threatens Ptolemy, and Ptolemy kills Alfred. After the shooting,
Ptolemy loses his newfound clarity. In the novel's final pages, he does not even
know his own name, and he barely remembers Robyn.

Ptolemy's primary battle is with nature and time; he is fighting to keep
control over his mind, and more specifically his memories, as he succumbs to
dementia and age. He wants most urgently, though, to remember what he did
with Coydog's treasure, and this treasure—as evidenced by Coydog's extensive
reflections on sin and judgment, especially regarding this illegal acquisition of
this treasure—links Ptolemy's battle with nature to the conflict between heaven
and hell, good and evil. In order to redeem himself and save his family, Ptolemy

must not only make a deal with "the devil" (Dr. Ruben), but also be willing to sacrifice his soul—just a Coydog did—by subverting God's unjust rules to instead follow Coydog's morality, exemplified by his "righteous crime" of stealing a slaveholder's fortune in order to redistribute it to oppressed African Americans. Even Ptolemy's nickname, "Pity," given to him "because Ptolemy seemed like blasphemy, though no one could say why," foreshadows this epic confrontation (8).

Before Robin and the devil's medicine, though, Ptolemy is desperately confused and hopelessly distanced from the memories he wants to access. They, like the secrets of Coydog's treasure, are lost. His thoughts, early in the novel, "were still his, still in the range of his thinking, but they were, many and most of them, locked on the other side of a closed door that he'd lost the key for. So, his memory became like secrets held away from his own mind" (12). The memories still haunt him, though, because "these secrets were noisy things; they babbled and muttered behind the door, and so if he listened closely he might catch a snatch of something he once knew well" (12). Most of his family, with the exception of his grandnephew Reggie, ignores him, and he has little to no sense of time or purpose.

Reggie's death devastates him, and the shock of the news pushes Ptolemy to create a connection between Reggie's death, Coydog's lynching, and a larger purpose he needs to fulfill. Still in a haze, "Ptolemy squinted, trying to see with his mind's eye the reasoning behind Reggie's murder," but rather than think immediately of Reggie, Ptolemy "remembered his hidden box and a promise he'd made to Coydog before the old man was dragged off and killed like some wild animal. It was something that happened to colored men and boys since they left the land of Ptolemy, father of Cleopatra" (44). Ptolemy, even with dementia, understands that the senseless violence that killed Reggie is fueled by the same hate and the same historical reality that fueled Coydog's lynching. The equation reminds Ptolemy, even just faintly, that he was destined to do something to counter that violence and thwart that hate.

Ptolemy's relationship with Robyn also bolsters his renewed purpose and clarity. Before Robin and the changes she helps him make, he realizes, "the content of his mind was the radio and the TV, that he was just as empty as an old cracked pecan shell—the meat dried up and crumbled away" (86). Robin is uniquely able to help him, though, because "Her almond-shaped eyes looked right into his, not making him feel old or like he wasn't there" (38). Robyn makes him feel like he has purpose and a reason to live: "She was his child, his baby girl. She needed his protection" (59). He tells her, "I'm a man dyin'a thirst an' you the on'y water in a thousand miles" (102).

Driven by the deep feelings that Reggie's death and Robin's care have inspired in him, as well as by his now overwhelming feeling that he must keep his promise to Coydog in order to fulfill his duty to Robin and Reggie, Ptolemy, like Tempest Landry, agrees to give his body to Dr. Reuben—Satan—in exchange for temporary control over his mind. When Dr. Reuben tells Ptolemy about the "cocktail" of medicine developed by "a group of physicians from all over the world" who "make it in a town in Southeast Asia where there are fewer laws governing research" and tells him honestly that the chances of relief or survival were questionable, Ptolemy immediately thinks of Coydog's metaphor comparing the devil to a bartender who serves up "your poison" (128). Coydog also taught Ptolemy that the lines between good and evil were not always clear: "Devil is an angel like the rest," so "you got to give him his due" (129). Even in confusion, though, Ptolemy is clear that he is not selling his soul; he will not accept any compensation for participating in the trial. He assures Robyn: "I done played the Devil an' beat him at his own game. On'y way he could take my soul is if he give to me. But I tricked him. I made a fair trade wit' him. I give 'im my body but not my soul" (131). Making a "trade" instead of taking a gift trades mind for body, so his "deal" with the devil does not involve his soul.

And Satan's medicine delivers the promised results, but while the medicine is working Ptolemy also feels like "he was burning alive" in "the Devil's fire" that "ignited him"—a hellfire that suggests damnation and parallels Ptolemy's slow death with Coydog's lynching (221). During Ptolemy's four-day-long unconscious fever spell after taking the first round of the medicine, *Los Angeles Times* critic Tim Rutten points out, "we get to know history not just in drifting fragment, but in chronology."[15] Ptolemy remembers and recounts the full story of the treasure and Coydog's instructions to "take that treasure and make a difference for poor black folks treated like they do us" (140). He does not just regain individual memory, but also a collective, historical memory. The devil's medicine, Ptolemy tells his family, "opened my mind all the way back to the first day I could remember as a child. I can think so clear that I could almost remember what my father's father was thinkin' the day he conceived my old man" (157).

In her review of the novel, *New York Times* critic Marilyn Stasio writes, "While Ptolemy's early ramblings are the sad songs of one lost mind, the memories he recovers, including barbaric acts he observed as the son of a Southern sharecropper, are the modern history of his people."[16] Now, however, he has control of that history and of his own destiny, and "now he carried the past with him rather than being carried on the back of the brute that was his history" (167).

In one of the later fever dreams, Coydog visits with the Ptolemy of the present: Coydog asks him why he waited for so long to use the treasure. Ptolemy tells Coydog he was "scared" because "there's blood on that gold," to which Coydog replies: "My blood. You know, for every grain of gold dust that make up that treasure a black mother have cried and a black son done shed sweat or blood, maybe even life itself" (241).

Realizing that he will not have the time to see the plans he's set in motion fully realized, he passes the responsibility on to Robyn, his "heir" both literally and metaphorically. In the opening "Afterword," he reminds her of this when he writes, "I want you to know that everybody in my family is counting on you" (1). Whereas Robyn's need for him initially gave him purpose, Ptolemy now looks to her "strength" to meet his family's needs. He tells her, "You the one gonna make Coy's dream into somethin' real" (210). Rather than align Robin with sin or the devil, though, Ptolemy instead makes her angelic. When he wakes from his fever dream and sees her watching over him, he twice calls her "a gift from God" (153). When she asserts that someone else would have stepped in to care for him if she had not, Ptolemy replies, "They'da come, but I still wouldn't be here. It's me that's the lump 'a clay and you that's the hand of God" (153).

He has no memory of his personal identity, but he retains his knowledge of fulfilling his commitment to his friend and community. He also still has Robyn—his personal agent of God—and an abstracted awareness of Coydog's continued companionship. As he looks around the room after his descent into amnesia, "he saw and registered and forgot many things on his way. The empty room and the green door and the feeling that he had accomplished an ancient task that had been behind a door and under a floor"; he also sees "the girl" who "was one of a kind, like the woman who had come to his door and yanked him out of his sad and lonely life" (276). He also then remembers her name, but has to ask his own. The dementia cannot take away the value of their connection nor Ptolemy's understanding of his role in helping his community. Similarly, even though Ptolemy cannot name his friend, as the novel closes he feels his presence as "a coyote that talked like a man whispered in his ear and then licked his face, and then . . ." (277). These images suggest, as his eminent death approaches, that murdering Alfred and keeping the white man's treasure have not damned him to hell's fire and isolation, but rather that his liberated and blameless soul will pass into an alternate consciousness defined by the love he deserves.

CHAPTER SEVEN

Nonfiction

Stories Come to Life

Although Walter Mosley's first book-length nonfiction piece, *Workin' on the Chain Gang: Shaking Off the Dead Hand of History* (2000), appeared ten years after his first novel, *Devil in A Blue Dress,* the compelling thematic connections between Mosley's fiction and nonfiction could almost lead readers to suspect that his most celebrated protagonists—including Easy Rawlins, Fearless Jones, Charles Blakey, and Leonid McGill—were sitting with Mosley as he wrote the nonfiction.

Mosley's nonfiction often takes the form of treatise, personal reflection, instruction manual, or a combination thereof. The major political works include *Workin' on the Chain Gang* (2000), *What Next: An African American Initiative Toward World Peace* (2003), *Life Out of Context: Which Includes a Proposal for the Non-violent Takeover of the House of Representatives* (2006), and *Twelve Steps Toward Political Revelation* (2011). Together, these provide an intensely personal mixture of biography and call to action. All, for example, recount stories or lessons from Mosley's father, all feature reflections on the writing process, and all challenge Americans—black Americans in particular—to unite in solidarity against hegemony, racism, and imperialism.

Mosley writes in *Life Out of Context*: "All political activity is based upon prosaic human experience. We get involved in politics to better our situation and possibly to help others. Accepting this notion as a given, I tried to connect my personal struggles with how I perceive political realities in the United States and beyond" (2).[1] To persuade his audience to act—be that action writing, humanitarian efforts, or social uprising—Mosley offers examples and lessons aimed at guiding readers through the same questions that inform his fiction:

What does it mean to be American? How does the answer differ for black and white citizens or for men and women? How can Americans remember the past but still transform the future? And most importantly, who will tell America's story in the twenty-first century?

Considering Mosley's fiction and nonfiction side by side highlights key personal and political elements in both and demonstrates the inevitable interconnectivity of life and art. The fiction introduces and illustrates the conflicts that the nonfiction explores; the fiction helps us feel and understand the past, which the nonfiction helps us apply to the present.

Workin' on the Chain Gang and A Red Death

Mosley's central argument in his first book-length nonfiction piece, *Workin' on the Chain Gang: Shaking Off the Dead Hand of History,* is that "the lack of a true understanding of African-American history and its relation to the rest of the American story keeps the whole nation from a clear understanding and articulation of the present-day political and economic problems that face all" (13).[2] Mosley does not advocate looking beyond race, but suggests using race as a lens for broader application because, by looking at the world through the lens of racialized experience, we understand all oppression better. He is "looking at race to provide a key to the problems that face all of us in America" (15) because all Americans have "inherited" chains: "The shackles of slavery, the restraints of capitalism, the corruption of idealistic systems, and the iron convictions of hatred—these are our baggage" (5).

"Money has," Mosley suggests, "formed the bonds of our imprisonment. Our labor binds us to a system that can see us only as units of value or expense" (6). All Americans are, in effect, slaves of the economic power structures: "We are all part of an economic machine. Some of us are cogs, others ghosts, but it is the machine, not race or gender or even nationality, that drives us" (12). To understand this de facto slavery and plot a response to it, then, Americans should look back to actual slavery and its aftermath and try to replicate the modes of rebellion that were effective against it. In the introduction to their collection of essays on Mosley's works, editors Owen E. Brady and Derek C. Maus posit that "widely shared consciousness of African American experience could, in Mosley's mind, help Americans move toward a more humane sense of home; recognizing one's solidarity with and identity as a kind of slave would provoke change or new ideas for the future."[3]

Workin' on the Chain Gang outlines these ideas in five main sections: the black experience in America as a torch in the darkness, the truth as a commodity and barometer for our own commitment to growth, the man in the mirror, defining the great enemy—the margin of profit, and Mosley's platform for the presidency. Of these concepts, Mosley says, "I hope these different contemplations on liberation will stimulate some thoughts about what might be in everyday life. Rather than answers, they are departure points meant to ignite the creation of a new world, at least in the mind of the thinker (you)" (36). He also acknowledges that his proposals might sound far-fetched, but challenges that "the only way out is to be crazy, to imagine the impossible and the ridiculous, to say what it is that you want in spite of everyone else's embarrassed laughs. This is a little easier for me because I am a fiction writer. Pushing ideas to their limit is what I'm expected to do—*in fiction*. But it's a small skip from fiction to nonfiction in this world of technology and change" (102–3).

And Mosley had "pushed" many of these same ideas in his fiction, especially in his 1991 novel, *A Red Death,* in which Easy Rawlins investigates a Jewish communist leader, Chaim Wenzler, during the Red Scare. Government agents initiate this investigation when they threaten Easy's property, and he is "so worried about my money and my freedom that I had become their slave" (124).[4] White America, Easy realizes, has the power to take away all of his resources and use that power to control his labor.

When Easy meets Wenzler, the leader explains that he has come to Watts to organize a political movement "because Negroes in America have the same life as the Jew in Poland. Ridiculed, segregated. We were hung and burned just for being alive" (91). Easy, too, expresses his understanding of shared suffering by paralleling violence against African Americans (lynching specifically) with the violence Jesus endured. Easy looks at the statue of Christ on the church and reflects, "I heard something, but it was like something in the back of my mind. Like a crackle of a lit match and the sigh of an old timber in a windstorm" (136). Both Wenzler and Easy see potential power in acknowledging the solidarity of shared suffering that Mosley describes in *Working on the Chain Gang.* Mosley writes, "Violence and oppression rob us of the ability to understand. Without understanding there can be no growth, no recognition of truth, and no tomorrow—only endless repetition of great todays" (16).

The strongest philosophical voice in *A Red Death,* though, is Jackson Blue's. Among Easy's oldest friends, Jackson is the smartest man he knows, and whenever Easy needs help sorting out a problem's logic, he turns to Jackson to talk him through it. In *A Red Death,* Easy asks Jackson, "What about these communists? What you think about them?" Jackson replies: "Well, Easy, that's easy," he said and laughed at how it sounded. "You know it's always the same old shit. You got yo' people already got a hold on sumpin' like money. An' you got yo' people ain't go nunthin' but they want sumpin' in the worst way. So the banker and the corporation man gots it all, an' the workin' man ain't got shit. Now the workin' man have a union to say that it's the work makes stuff so he should be gettin' the money. That like com'unism. But the rich man don't like it so he gonna break the worker's back" (197).

Jackson, like Mosley in *Working on the Chain Gang,* believes that "the value of life itself fluctuates according to the cost of production" (11), and even beyond this, that "margin of profit, among other things, defines our labor; more, it defines our humanity. The job you hold, the income you bring home, the recognition of your value to society, are deeply informed by your labors" (90).

Jackson also discusses Africa, which he links to communism through W. E. B. DuBois. Easy had not heard of DuBois, so Jackson explains, "He's a famous Negro, Easy. Almost a hundred years old. He's always writin' 'bout gettin' back t' Africa. You prob'ly ain't never heard'a him 'cause he's a com'unist. They don't teach ya 'bout com'unists" (184–85). When Easy then asks, "So how do you know, if they don't teach it, "Jackson replies, "Lib'ary got its do' open, man. Ain't nobody tellin' you not to go" (185). Jackson's nationalistic ideas, combined with his vernacular speech, highlight the everyday value of the stories that are excluded from dominant histories.

These sentiments in general, and the nod to DuBois in particular, also foreshadow the sentiments in *Working on the Chain Gang* because the treatise pays not-so-subtle homage to DuBois's vision for the "Talented Tenth." Although DuBois was not the first to use the term, he arguably used it most famously. In his 1903 essay "The Talented Tenth," published in Booker T. Washington's collection *The Negro Problem,* DuBois wrote, "The Negro race, like all races, is going to be saved by its exceptional men. The problem of education, then, among Negroes must first of all deal with the Talented Tenth; it is the problem of developing the Best of this race that they may guide the Mass away from the contamination and death of the Worst, in their own and other races."[5] He goes on to suggest, "The Talented Tenth of the Negro race must be made leaders of thought and missionaries of culture among their people."[6]

In *Working on the Chain Gang,* Mosley similarly posits that "at least ten percent of the population" needs to question what they are "owed" by the system. He adds, "Ten percent is an arbitrary number. I'm simply saying that the number of people that it takes to make political change is actually quite small. A fraction of the populace that is sure of what changes are necessary can change the minds of their neighbors" (90). Even if the numeric link to DuBois is "arbitrary," the conceptual connections between the two men's ideas underscore Mosley's argument that the social and economic struggles that he interrogates in *Workin' on the Chain Gang* are ongoing, even timeless.

Just as Easy Rawlins finds unexpected allies in communities across Los Angeles during his investigations in *A Red Death,* Mosley does not specify the racial heritage of his 10 percent in *Working on the Chain Gang,* and in his foreword to the 2006 edition, Clyde Taylor points to Mosley's purposely broad audience as a key element in the text's rhetorical strategy. Taylor argues, "It's a kind of revolutionary act to write this way, directing language to an expensively educated gentrifier or a welfare mother or a teenage son of immigrants alike, all reading the same thing, and maybe sharing the same thoughts" (vii).

What Next and Fearless Jones

Mosley dedicates his second nonfiction text—which was released after the September 11, 2001, terrorist attacks and the start of the second Gulf War—to Haki Madhubuti, "poet, educator, activist, father, and man." *What Next: A Memoir Toward World Peace* opens with a note explaining that, although "everyone is invited to read this book," the target audience is African Americans because, Mosley explains, "it is a reflection on our history and subsequently our future" (7).[7] Also, as in *Working on the Chain Gang*, Mosley suggests that African American history and experience are an invaluable lens for understanding current events because African Americans "have a singular perspective on the qualities of revenge, security, and peace that will positively inform that direction of our nation's sometimes ill-considered standards" (7).

Mosley opens with a discussion of his father's experience as a soldier in World War II and a reflection on the value of his father's stories. His father's "great treasury of tales," Mosley explains, held the "remedy" for mistakes (12). He then reflects on how his father's stories and experience apply to the post-9/11 world. In particular, Mosley writes of "the frightening moment when I realized that I was on one side of the conflict, that the men who destroyed those buildings saw me as their enemy too" (21). For the terrorists, there was no black America or white America. And this awakening leads him to conclude that "black men and women in every stratum of American society" share America's global responsibilities because they "live in and are a part of an economic system of terror" (26). Even though they are, themselves, "descendants of human suffering," they are now "living in a fine mansion at the edge of a precipice. And the ground is caving in under the weight of our wealth and privilege" (26).

With this history and this privilege comes the responsibility to speak out against oppression, especially when that oppression is sanctioned by the government that African Americans support—socially and financially. Mosley outlines four "rules of fair treatment": "First, I cannot be free while my neighbor is wearing chains / Second, I cannot know happiness while others are forced to live in despair / Third, I cannot know health if plague and famine thrive outside my door / and last, but not least, I cannot expect to know peace if war rides forward under my flag and with my consent" (41). Mosley even encourages his audience to question and challenge the ideas in his own text.

Mosley goes on to outline the reasons why America's enemies should simply be "all persons involved in causing the deaths of others—either actively or from a consciously passive posture—for political, nationalistic, or economic ends" (51), and he explores the potential reasons why the United States has become an enemy to millions of people who see Americans as controlling and as "economic invaders" (54). Pointing out, as he suggested in *Working on the Chain Gang,* that "America's foreign policy has been based on ensuring profitability for the nation's businesses, not democracy for the masses," Mosley urges African Americans to question their potential role "in creating that evil, that insanity," that characterizes terrorism (60–61). Concerned that Condoleezza Rice and Colin Powell have come to "represent" black political thought, he encourages African Americans to resist silence and instead "stand up and enter the dialogue about the War in the Middle East," lest they become "enmeshed in a logic of violence and murder" that would be "on equal par with the slave-masters of old" (84–85).

Most of all, though, Mosley says that Americans need "conviction to create harmony in the world" in order to find "world peace" (98). He believes that a change in attitude and a grassroots conviction to celebrate and promote democracy would be a more powerful force against hate and violence than any weapon that any country could create. Specifically, Mosley wants to create an "African-American led peace movement" (106) that uses a combination of media, small discussion groups, and political action to change the global balance of power and "put ourselves in the true position of greatness by making a world where life is sensible, sacred, and sure of its moral atmosphere" (136). As the African American Literature Book Club review summarizes, "*What Next* is a command not a plea, and Mosley's between-the-lines message is really where the action is: Forget about fear and apply our energies, resources and good will to ensuring that everyone around the world gets a fair shake."[8]

Fearless Jones, the first novel in Mosley's second mystery series, follows the title character and his best friend, narrator Paris Minton, as they try to solve a series of murders connected to Nazi thefts during World War II. *What Next*'s first connection to *Fearless Jones* is military service. Fearless recalls, "I was in a war eight thousand miles from home with white men talkin' German in front 'a me an' white men talkin' English at my back. They was all callin' me nigger. They all wanted me dead" (117).[9] Similarly, of his experience in World War II, Leroy Mosley recounts, "[The Germans] shooting at me was what made me realize that I really was an American. That's why, when I was discharged, I left the South and came here to Los Angeles. Because I couldn't live among people who didn't know or couldn't accept what I become in danger and under fire in the war" (10). Writing down his father's account of these experiences decades after they happened, Walter Mosley becomes fascinated with this disconnect and how the people that are trying to take someone's life can actually define that life. While Leroy Mosley has a less racially antagonistic relationship with the Germans—they just want to kill him because he's American—both share the racialized rejection on the home front, suggesting that racism makes America, especially the American South, into a battlefield that is just as formidable as the bloody German front.

While serving in Germany, Fearless also liberated Nazi concentration camps, so when his Jewish friend Fanny recounts her family's and friends' experiences in the camps, both Fearless and his sidekick Paris feel a kinship with her—Fearless because of his experience and Paris because of the historical connection between the camps and slave quarters. Paris explains, "No black man liked the notion of concentration camps; we have lived in labor camps the first 250 years of our residence in America. And for Fearless it was even worse; he had actually seen the camps" (290–91). This type of empathy is at the core of Mosley's question/call to action in *What Next*: "How can we, Black people of America, who have suffered so much under the iron heel of progress, stand back and allow people to starve and die as silently and unheralded as our own ancestors did on those slave ships so many years ago?" (37). Harkening back to his arguments in *Working on the Chain Gang*, Mosley again points out the value of using the black experience—past and present—as a lens for clarifying events and responsibilities—present and future.

Fearless Jones's reflections on war and the "enemy" foreshadow the indictments that Mosley issues in *What Next*. As Paris and Fearless run from a murder, Fearless tells Paris, "You know I promised myself a long time ago that I wasn't gonna put myself back in a war for nuthin', not even America. [. . .] This right here is war, baby [. . .] And where my own country couldn't make me—you did" (220–21). Here, Fearless suggest that in war the enemy and the aims are not always clear, and his sadness in this scene suggests that those fighting in wars are not always willing participants.

On this topic, Mosley writes in *What Next*, "We must seriously consider the possibility that we number among the ranks of The Enemy. If we can blame a group of people as a whole because their representatives use the tools of killers, then how can we exonerate ourselves if our deputies use the same methods?" (52). This question, like Fearless's observation, suggests that, in war, who is fighting and why are not always clear. Fearless, for example, imagines that he is helping his friends, but he suddenly finds himself on the metaphorical battlefield. Similarly, soldiers in armed conflicts believe that they are defending their homes and their way of life, but they may also realize that they have become part of a larger conflict that no that longer aligns with their beliefs or convictions.

Life Out of Context and *The Man in My Basement*

Written in "a feverish episode," *Life out of Context: Which Includes a Proposal for the Non-violent Takeover of the House of Representatives* aims "to uncover and articulate methods we could employ to make the world safer for the millions who are needlessly suffering" (1). The slim reflection, dedicated to New York poet and novelist Donna Masini, promises to be "a political work" from a nonexpert perspective "anchored in some very personal and even pedestrian experiences" (1). The result, according to *International Socialist Review* commentator Keeanga-Yamahtta Taylor, is a text that is "part political call-to-arms, part cynical lamentation, and part cathartic rant about the state of the world and the state of American politics."[10]

In the first of these experiences Mosley describes, he describes attending an event at which he encounters a writer who he believes thrives off situating himself in very a specific, very comfortable, and very narrow "cultural, intellectual, artistic, and professional context" (6); this encounter leads to a series of reflections on "contexts," and Mosley ultimately realizes that he feels "oppressed by this notion of a literary context" because he does not feel like he has his own context (9). Mosley is able to accept this lack, though, and he is reinvigorated and refocused first by watching a documentary—Manthia Diawara's *Conakry Kas,* which addresses "the multifaceted character of Africa—and then by listening to (after introducing) a talk between former actor turned activist Harry Belafonte and South African jazz artist Hugh Masekela, moderated by poet Quincy Troupe (11).

Mosley chronicles his anxieties about writing the introduction for the event. He describes his writing process and how the anxiety brought up memories of being harassed by white cops as a child. With the introduction behind him, though, he is freed to be moved by the conversation. Masekela shows him the possibility that "South Africa is the hope of the world" (29), and Mosley observes, "The context of our struggle has an ancient cast to it" (31). Harry Belafonte's points about "the failure of the civil rights movement" then start Mosley thinking, "We might have to see ourselves outside the context of our ex-slavehood and civil rights in a world where murder has taken the place of diplomacy" (36–37).

Although the Masekela-Belafonte event profoundly inspires him and pushes him to think more deeply about context, the concrete answers he craves—especially as the concept pertains to class and wealth—still elude Mosley. He tries to "crystallize the notion into a rallying call, slogan, or motto," but realizes that he must first consider "the threats facing Americans at large and Black America in particular" (45). Then he is further demoralized by the feeling that "there are too many issues and not one of them, it seemed, was compelling enough to move a nation" (46). This realization leads Mosley to reflect on the limits of language, especially for creating sympathy for, and inspiring action on, global human rights issues. He also questions how, then, to move beyond language to create and inspire.

As a response to these questions, Mosley "[moves] toward advocacy of grassroots citizen action" [11] and envisions a large-scale media and internet campaign with electronic billboards and corresponding Web sites, but he also envisions smaller-scale political changes, including the formation of a Black Party, focused on African American interests (57). This Black Party, he posits, "could actually democratize America by taking the power away from the two-party system and handing it over to the people" (58). While Mosley also makes clear that he does not want to be the leader of this "political unit," he does provide a list of party "demands," which include "a commitment to revamping the legal system and the penal system" and "a universal health-care system" (60–61).

Whatever path Americans take, they must overtly challenge their leaders and the morality of those leaders' actions. Mosley believes that "we are living a life out of context with our own belief systems, with what we believe to be good and right" (69). Part of the solution, he believes, is stronger leaders, and he calls on his younger readers to step up. He also calls on artists and cultural luminaries to make sure that African Americans are "represented when the white world gets together to construct policies and give out awards for excellence" lest exclusion remain the unchallenged norm (84). In sum, he writes, "It is time for us to pull ourselves into context" (86). The process will certainly be arduous and complicated, and while Mosley does not guarantee that his plan will ultimately solve all of the world's ills, he does believe it at least "will lead somewhere" (104).

The Man in My Basement (2004), one of Mosley's most popular non-mystery fictions, chronicles the relationship between a floundering black man, Charles Blakey, and the rich white man, Anniston Bennet, who rents Blakey's basement to imprison himself for his past crimes, especially crimes in Africa. The first clue that there is significant thematic overlap between *The Man in My Basement* and *Life Out of Context* is that the novel is dedicated to Harry Belafonte, "the man of the world." On a larger scale, though, Mosley's feeling that he does not have a place, or context, in the literary world, echoes *The Man in My Basement*'s protagonist Charles's sense that he does not have a place in his world because of his lack of connections to his family and cultural history.

As Charles begins to connect with his African heritage, though, he begins to find purpose, and part of that purpose is to help the world understand justice and expressions of human value. In a heated conversation with African art historian Narciss, Charles argues: "But standing on the outside quoting Engels and Marx isn't going to help. Sayin' *that's not fair* won't do anything either. What I want is to find out, to get in there and see for myself. Because you know they aren't going to stop doing what they're doing just because we whisper something against them at night on the phone. I mean, I put gas in my tank, don't I? That's what voting is to big business, you know. It's not a secret ballot; it's a purchase. If you buy from him, that's your vote of confidence" (158).[12] At this point in the novel, Charles is beginning to understand the forces that determine the value of human life—as labor, as soldiers, as consumers, and beyond—and beginning to see the role that Americans play in global exploitation, even when Americans are not physically in the factories or the fields where that exploitation takes place.

Mosley himself is enacting Charles's mandate through the act of writing *Life Out of Context* and participating in the events it describes, but he also sees similar ideas interrogated in *Conakry Kas*. He reports, "The Africans I'd seen in Professor Diawara's film were elements in many different and conflicting contexts. Young people at risk and impoverished in a world that knows nothing about them and that cares even less," they are "waiting for the world to see their worth and just about out of time. Brilliant, beautiful, and tragic, they are my brothers and sisters who cannot move in harmony because their world has been made dissonant by so many foreign and international pressures" (15). Africa is one of the sites of exploitation that Charles has in mind during his conversation with Narciss because Charles's basement "prisoner," Bennet, confesses to conducting many nefarious dealings there. The key for the world to see the worth that the film describes is for Americans to understand how they are "voting" for a specific valuation of human life based on how they cast their "ballots" at the gas pump and elsewhere.

In order to achieve full awareness of global issues, though, African Americans need to find self-awareness—a knowledge of their status at home and how understanding that status can inform more global observations. In *The Man in My Basement,* Charles describes the moment when he realizes that "it was as if everybody had become like a mirror, and I saw reflections of what they saw instead of what it was they were trying to show me or tell me[. . . .] And when I saw or heard something I did not like, I had the chance to alter my behavior" (208). Charles sees redemptive potential in this riff on DuBoisian double-consciousness.[13]

However, in *Life Out of Context,* Mosley reasserts the potentially negative consequences of this divided self, especially on the ability to understand identity in a racialized context. Mosley uses the example of being stopped by the police for riding his bike on the wrong side of town. In this moment, he asserts, "You see yourself and other Black people the way the police and the courts and the schools and the banks see you. You are guilty in their eyes until you prove otherwise" (26).

The most important concept linking these two texts, though, is incarceration. Bennet imprisons himself in the novel, but Charles quickly becomes an oppressor who "dominated him with the fear of isolation" (242). This reversal becomes more stunning and more significant in the context of Mosley's background on black incarceration rates in *Life Out of Context*. He reports, "At any given moment there are a million people of color in American prisons. Add to that the millions that have been temporarily released only to find themselves back within the system in a few years' time, and you have a method of oppression that goes along unchecked and, even worse, unexamined" (31). And perhaps imagining someone just like Charles, Mosley, as he listens to Belafonte speak, thinks, "We might have to see that we have been occupying the role of oppressor instead of the oppressed" (36–37).

Twelve Steps Toward Political Revelation and *The Long Fall*

Mosley's most recent nonfiction work, *Twelve Steps Toward Political Revelation*, is subtitled "the potential for an American epiphany under the rough blanket of capitalism," although this subtitle is not printed on the cover, as it was in the previous nonfiction works; it appears only on the title page. Mosley begins the work with a prefatory note, explaining a key distinction between this text and Karl Marx's *Capital*. Mosley believes Marx's decision to name his rich man "Mr. Moneybags" was ultimately misguided because "the term removes the capitalist from the constructs of history that necessarily formed him" (ix–x).[14] So Mosley calls his rich group "The Joes," to mark them as "regular people" who just have more money (ix).

This distinction sets the tone for the revolutionary ideas that follow. Mosley establishes that "this book is an exploration into the ways in which we are oppressed (along with the possibilities of overthrowing the tyranny) in our everyday lives" (xi). He believes that "the systems and institutions of this nation place heavy loads and hidden addictions on our bodies and minds at the earliest possible age and then expect us to labor under these weights from childhood until the day we die" (xi). "Admirably candid about his own struggles,"[15] he parallels his experiences with substance abuse and addiction with "another form of dependence: Americanism," which is "a belief-system as absolute as any cult or mania" (xvi). Mosley's *Twelve Steps*, then, is akin to a twelve-step program to combat addiction—in this case, "the emotional and economically based addictions that lay claim to almost every aspect of our lives" (xvi).

The only step, however, that directly mirrors the twelve steps Alcoholics Anonymous developed is the first one: admitting there is a problem and

defining that problem; beyond this, Mosley's steps are generally original and
focused on the personal, psychological, financial, and logistical elements of the
proposed revolution against the metaphorical addiction. Step one—"getting
a handle on the definitions and interconnection of our afflictions and addictions"—might, he claims, "be the greatest conundrum we ever face" (1). After
this initial definition, Americans must find a common language and common
texts, ideally through a "universal education" plan he outlines, and they must
commit "to tell the truth at least once a day"; Mosley provides tangible tips for
how to do this as well (18).

Other steps in the plan are more financially focused. Mosley writes in step
four—defining the classes—"We are, in part, defined by how we are organized
inside, and against the underbelly of, the economic system" (25); it is only
through understanding the class labels that categorize, and therefore divide,
that Americans can "come together in political solidarity" (30). He explains
further in step eight—attempting to understand the mind in relation to the
economic infrastructure—that while he does not see himself as "a proponent
of psychoanalysis proper" or as a Marxist, he is proposing "a kind of Marx-
ian Psychoanalysis" that interrogates the ways in which American approaches
to labor, wealth, and class construct American lives and "the bugaboos in our
minds" (60).

Psychotherapy, therefore, is an integral element of Mosley's steps because
"we need treatment for our infected souls" as well as more self-awareness (39).
Echoing the personal and moral "inventories" that traditional twelve-step
programs embrace, Mosley suggests some kind of daily self check-in, ideally
through writing. He explains, "Every day you have to sit with your self and try
to figure out what is right and what is wrong in your life. You need to write
these ideas down, consider them, edit them, then rewrite them. The world will
not change without you changing" (46). The goal, as in any addiction program,
is "personal recovery," and an acceptance of individual, as well as social and
economic, "value" (82).

In the final step—defining and claiming genius—Mosley calls his audience,
"a populace beaten down by economic turmoil and deceitful leaders,"[16] to not
only recognize this value, but also to collaborate to increase its global impact.
He urges, "We the people, are the genius. We are repositories of thousands
of years of language, wisdom, and hard knocks. When we come together in
a sublime cultural epiphany: That's when there is potential and growth" (85).
Specifically, he suggests small discussion groups (of a dozen people) who meet
regularly to discuss the issues and their ideas about them. These "Meetings of
the Twelve" can then go "viral" and help "exercise real democratic processes"
with national as well as international implications (91–92).

Mosley's most recent detective, Leonid McGill, debuted in *The Long Fall* (2009). In this mystery, Leonid investigates the murder of a young man he unwittingly exposed by working for an anonymous client. Leonid has recently given up the criminal life, so his story also chronicles his continued attempts to subvert the elements of that life that threaten to drag him back. Leonid not only struggles with various addictions—linking his story to *Twelve Steps*'s central metaphor—but he also trained to be a boxer after he was orphaned by the death of his ill mother and the disappearance of his Marxist father. *Twelve Steps*'s extended boxing metaphor also evokes Leonid's personal narrative, which often parallels Leonid's experience in training with his experiences on the street as a private investigator.

Mosley writes in *Twelve Steps* about a boxing match between the Everyday Denizens and the Joes. He explains that this match "might be skill versus brute power, reach versus close-to-the-ground weight, determination versus self confidence, or just the power of one opponent to psych out the other. These rivals will be more or less evenly matched (because the fight is the thing: the debacle that is our *open* market)" (75). The problem, Mosley explains, is that the rich, the Joes, control every tangible aspect of the fight—from ring size to the audience reaction.

The boxing-ring metaphor is important for both Leonid and the Denizens because, even though the ring is a confined and constructed space, it is subject to myriad influences, any one of which could substantially affect a match's outcome. Rather than simplify the number or the extent of possible outcomes, the confined ring magnifies those outcomes. Leonid uses boxing as a metaphor for his past and for his complex cases, but the applicability of that model to politics and economics suggests that such microcosmic analysis can provide helpful "worse-case scenario" results that are likely but also, unfortunately, very disheartening.

Both Leonid and Mosley, though, see redemptive potential in literacy. Leonid expresses his sentiments through an extended description of librarians. Leonid believes "Librarians are wonderful people, partly because they are, on the whole, unaware of how dangerous knowledge is. Karl Marx upended the political landscape of the twentieth century sitting at a library table. Sill, modern librarians are more afraid of ignorance than they are of the potential devastation that knowledge can bring" (212).[17] Mosley, in *Twelve Steps,* writes, "Our teachers are overwhelmed and undereducated, while many parents are overworked and disengaged. Students are almost completely unaware of the empowerment that true education and literacy offer (9). While both *The Long Fall* and *Twelve Steps* acknowledge literacy's power, the fiction imagines literacy as a destructive power—it is "dangerous" and can wreak "potential

devastation"—whereas the nonfiction imagines literacy as creative, empower-
ing. Taken together, then, the two texts show the full range of literacy's transformative potential.

Reading is also the site of another convergence between these two texts:
a shared emphasis on political dishonesty, especially about the Iraq War. As
Leonid overhears a father chastising his young son, he starts reading the newspaper, "looking for an article to distract me" (229). He is immensely deflated to
realize, though, "The front page was the kind of triple obscenity" (229). First,
"The main story was about some Midwestern governor arrested by the FBI for
paying prostitutes to cross state lines"; then, "the nearby article said that the
Left was claiming that the death toll in Iraq was nearing a million while, by
some calculations, we would end up spending a trillion dollars on the effort.
That meant, by the end of our Middle Eastern folly, that you have spent a
million dollars for each death" (229). Expressing the same frustration, *Twelve
Steps* summarizes, "The reasons for the war we are fighting in Iraq are based
on lies. Our banks, our insurance and investment companies, all lied about
our money. Our religious and political leaders lie about their private lives with
almost predicable regularity" (18).

Although both the fiction and nonfiction again express the same frustration, the nonfiction legitimizes, or validates, the fiction's account: the newspaper in the novel is not, in fact, fiction. The fiction, though, can take liberties
to expand the context of this information and thus help readers better see its
applicability to their lives. For example, the third obscenity that Leonid feels as
he reads the paper is, he laments, that "it reminded me so much of the kind of
work I had once done to bring down otherwise good men" (229). In addition,
Leonid is struck by the callousness of the father that he is trying to "tune out"
with his reading, and they eventually fight. After this fight, Leonid muses, "it
seems that there was a whole world of wounded, half-conscious sires picking
fights and losing them" (232).

By linking the text of the newspaper to Leonid and the young father's
personal failures and regrets, the novel, like *Twelve Steps,* can suggest ways in
which a culture of lies shapes individual choices. As potent and mind-numbing
as any drug that an addict could seek out, the lies lead to more lies until everyone is fighting, but no one is sure why.

NOTES

Chapter One—Understanding Walter Mosley

1. Stefan Bradley, "Mosley, Walter," in *Encyclopedia of African American History, 1896 to the Present: From the Age of Segregation to the Twenty-first Century*, ed. Paul Finkelman (New York: Oxford University Press, 2008), www.oxfordaasc.com.libproxy .lib.unc.edu/article/opr/t0005/e0839 (accessed July 1, 2014).

2. Charles E. Wilson, *Walter Mosley: A Critical Companion* (Santa Barbara, CA: Greenwood, 2003), 2–5, ebooks.abc-clio.com.libproxy.lib.unc.edu/reader.aspx?isbn=97 80313058271&id=GR2022–106 (accessed July 1, 2014).

3. Ann Hostetler, "Mosley, Walter," in *African American National Biography*, ed. Henry Louis Gates Jr. and Evelyn Brooks Higginbotham (New York: Oxford UP, 2008), www.oxfordaasc.com.libproxy.lib.unc.edu/article/opr/t0001/e1667 (accessed May 20, 2014).

4. Wilson, *Walter Mosley: A Critical Companion*, 7–8.

5. Hostetler, "Mosley, Walter."

6. Wilson, *Walter Mosley: A Critical Companion*, 8.

7. Ibid., 9.

8. Johanna Neumann, "The Curious Case of Walter Mosley," *Moment*, September–October 2010, www.momentmag.com/the-curious-case-of-walter-mosley/ (accessed December 1, 2014).

9. Amy Goodman, "Author Walter Mosley on Writing Mystery Novels, Political Revelation, Racism and Pushing Obama," *Democracy Now!* February 27, 2012, www .democracynow.org/2012/2/27/author_walter_mosley_on_writing_mystery (accessed March 1, 2014).

10. Quoted in Juan F. Elices, "Shadows of an Eminent Future," in *Finding a Way Home: A Critical Assessment of Walter Mosley's Fiction*, ed. Owen E. Brady and Derek C. Maus (Jackson: University Press of Mississippi, 2008), 133, site.ebrary.com.libproxy.lib .unc.edu/lib/uncch/detail.action?docID=10282590 (accessed March 12, 2014).

11. Wilson, *Walter Mosley: A Critical Companion*, 33.

12. Owen E. Brady and Derek C. Maus, "Epilogue: Wither Walter? A Brief Overview of Walter Mosley's Recent Work," in *Finding a Way Home*, ed. Brady and Maus, 161.

13. Andrew Pepper, "'The Fire This Time': Social Protest and Racial Politics from Himes to Mosley," in *The Contemporary American Crime Novel: Race Ethnicity Gender Class* (Chicago: Fitzroy-Dearborn Press, 2001), Google Books edition (accessed March 1, 2014), 110.

14. D. J. R. Bruckner, "Mystery Stories Are Novelist's Route To Moral Questions," *New York Times*, September 4, 1990, www.nytimes.com/1990/09/04/books/mystery-stories-are-novelist-s-route-to-moral-questions.html (accessed March 1, 2014).

15. Walter Mosley, *Life Out of Context: Which Includes a Proposal for the Non-violent Takeover of the House of Representatives* (New York: Avalon, 2006), 9.

16. Nicholas Kristof, "Professors, We Need You!" *New York Times,* February 15, 2014, www.nytimes.com/2014/02/16/opinion/sunday/kristof-professors-we-need-you.html?_r=0 (accessed March 15, 2014).

17. Walter Mosley, *This Year You Write Your Novel* (New York: Little Brown, 2007). Parenthetical citations of the book in this chapter refer to this edition.

Chapter Two—Easy's Evolution

1. "Covering Mosley: The Books of Walter Mosley," *New Yorker,* January 19, 2004, www.newyorker.com/magazine/2004/01/19/covering-mosley (accessed March 1, 2014).

2. Walter Mosley, *A Red Death* (New York: Pocket, 1992). All parenthetical citations of the book in this chapter refer to this edition.

3. Walter Mosley, *White Butterfly* (New York: Pocket, 1993). All parenthetical citations of the book in this chapter refer to this edition.

4. Roger A. Berger, "'The Black Dick': Race, Sexuality, and Discourse in the L.A. Novels of Walter Mosley," *African American Review* 31.2 (1997): 288.

5. Walter Mosley, *Gone Fishin'* (New York: Pocket, 1998). All parenthetical citations of the book in this chapter refer to this edition.

6. Walter Mosley, *A Little Yellow Dog* (New York: Washington Square Press, 2002). All parenthetical citations of the book in this chapter refer to this edition.

7. Walter Mosley, *Little Scarlet* (Boston: Little, Brown, 2004). All parenthetical citations of the book in this chapter refer to this edition.

8. Walter Mosley, *Blonde Faith* (New York: Grand Central, 2008). All parenthetical citations of the book in this chapter refer to this edition.

9. Walter Mosley, *Little Green* (New York: Doubleday, 2013). All parenthetical citations of the book in this chapter refer to this edition.

10. Marilyn C. Wesley, "'Power and Knowledge in Walter Mosley's *Devil in a Blue Dress*," *African American Review* 35.1 (2001): 108.

11. Walter Mosley, *Devil in a Blue Dress* (New York: Pocket, 1991). All parenthetical citations of the book in this chapter refer to this edition.

12. Walter Mosley, *Black Betty* (New York: Pocket, 1995). All parenthetical citations of the book in this chapter refer to this edition.

13. Walter Mosley, *Bad Boy Brawly Brown* (New York: Grand Central, 2008). All parenthetical citations of the book in this chapter refer to this edition.

14. Walter Mosley, *Cinnamon Kiss* (New York: Little, Brown, 2005). All parenthetical citations of the book in this chapter refer to this edition.

15. Nicole King, "'You Think Like You White': Questioning Race and Racial Community through the Lens of Middle-Class Desire(s)," *Novel: A Forum On Fiction* 35.2–3 (2002): 222.

16. W. E. B. DuBois, *The Souls of Black Folk* (New York: Norton, 1999), 10–11.

17. W. H. Auden, "The Guilty Vicarage: Notes on the Detective Story, by an Addict," *Harper's,* May 1948, 409.

18. Ibid.

19. Raymond Chandler, "The Simple Art of Murder," in *The Longman Anthology of Detective Fiction*, ed. Deane Mansfield-Kelley and Lois Marchino (New York: Pearson, 2005), 219.

20. Ibid.

21. Richard Bernstein, "Dark Street, Stolen Goods, and a Hard-bitten Dame," review of *Fearless Jones, New York Times,* July 2, 2001, www.nytimes.com/2001/07/02/books/books-of-the-times-dark-streets-stolen-goods-and-a-hard-bitten-dame.html (accessed July 1, 2014).

22. Maureen T. Reddy, "Race And American Crime Fiction," in *The Cambridge Companion to American Crime Fiction,* ed. Catherine Ross Nickerson (New York: Cambridge, 2010), 135–47, gateway.proquest.com.libproxy.lib.unc.edu/openurl?ctx_ver=Z39.88 –2003&xri:pqil:res_ver=0.2&res_id=xri:lion&rft_id=xri:lion:ft:criticism:R04647284:0 (accessed on July 1, 2014).

Chapter Three—Becoming Fearless

1. Nathaniel Hawthorne, "Ethan Brand: A Chapter from an Abortive Romance," in *The Complete Novels and Selected Tales of Nathaniel Hawthorne,* ed. Norman Holmes Pearson (New York: Random House, 1937), 1189.

2. Walter Mosley, *Fearless Jones* (New York: Warner Books, 2002). All parenthetical citations of the book in this chapter refer to this edition.

3. Jerrilyn McGregory, "Fearless Ezekiel: Alterity in the Detective Fiction of Walter Mosley," in *Finding a Way Home,* ed. Brady and Maus, 93.

4. Jesse Berrett, "Same Time, Same Place," review of *Fearless Jones, New York Times,* June 10, 2001, www.nytimes.com/books/01/06/10/reviews/010610.10berr.html (accessed July 1, 2014).

5. Bernstein, "Dark Street, Stolen Goods, and a Hard-bitten Dame."

Chapter Four—New York, New History, New Detective

1. Quoted in Mokoto Rich, "Walter Mosley's Three-Book Deal," *New York Times,* December 11, 2007, www.nytimes.com/2007/12/11/arts/11arts-WALTERMOSLEY_BRF.html?_r=0 (accessed March 1, 2014).

2. Walter Mosley, *The Long Fall* (New York: New American Library, 2010). All parenthetical citations of the book in this chapter refer to this edition.

3. Oline Codgill, "Life Not Easy for Leonid McGill," review of *The Long Fall, Sun Sentinel,* April 5, 2009, articles.sun-sentinel.com/2009–04–05/features/0904020263_1_easy-rawlins-private-detective-walter-mosley (accessed March 1, 2014).

4. Kevin Nance, "Leonid McGill, Walter Mosley's Post-black Hero, Returns," review of *All I Did Was Shoot My Man, Washington Post,* January 20, 2012, www.washingtonpost.com/lifestyle/style/leonid-mcgill-walter-mosleys-post-black-hero-returns/2012/01/17/gIQAj9EEEQ_story.html (accessed March 1, 2014).

5. Melinda Miller, "Walter Mosley Offers His Take on Politics, Race and Threats to Planet Earth," *Buffalo News,* February 24, 2013, www.buffalonews.com/20130224/walter_mosley_offers_his_take_on_politics_race_and_threats_to_planet_earth.html (accessed March 1, 2014).

6. Riverhead Books, *"The Long Fall* by Walter Mosley," www.youtube.com/watch?v=meKgcslIcbA (accessed December 1, 2014).

7. Ibid.

8. Carol Memmott, "Mosley's Hero in 'The Long Fall' is Easy to Like," *USA Today,* March 27, 2009, usatoday30.usatoday.com/life/books/reviews/2009-03-25-mosley -review_N.htm.

9. Riverhead Books, "*The Long Fall* by Walter Mosley."

Chapter Five—Mysterious Genres

1. Walter Mosley, *Blue Light* (Boston: Little Brown, 1998). All parenthetical citations of the book in this chapter refer to this edition.

2. Mel Watkins, "Primary Color," review of *Blue Light, New York Times,* November 15, 1998, www.nytimes.com/books/98/11/15/reviews/981115.15watkint.html (accessed November 1, 2014).

3. Houston A. Baker, *Blues, Ideology, and Afro-American Literature: A Vernacular Theory* (Chicago: University of Chicago Press, 1984), 3.

4. Ibid., 5.

5. Wilson, *Walter Mosley: A Critical Companion,* 154.

6. Ibid.

7. Elices, "Shadows of an Eminent Future," 136.

8. Water Mosley, *Diablerie* (New York: Bloomsbury, 2008). All parenthetical citations of the book in this chapter refer to this edition.

9. Brady and Maus, "Epilogue," in *Finding a Way Home,* ed. Brady and Maus, 163.

10. Renée Graham, "'Diablerie' Dives into Depths of Darkness," review of *Diablerie, Boston Globe,* January 24, 2008, www.boston.com/ae/books/articles/2008/01/24/diablerie_dives_into_depths_of_darkness/ (accessed November 1, 2014).

11. Reginald Martin, "Introduction: Dark Eros and the Erotic Essence," in *Dark Eros: Black Erotic Writings,* ed. Reginald Martin (New York: St. Martin's, 1997), xvi.

12. Elisabeth Vincentelli, "Walter Mosley Goes the Mickey Spillane Route," review of *Diablerie, Los Angeles Times,* July 19, 2008, articles.latimes.com/2008/jan/19/entertainment/et-book19 (accessed November 1, 2014).

Chapter Six—Hero or Villain?

1. Walter Mosley, *Twelve Steps Toward Political Revelation* (New York: Nation, 2011), 16.

2. Keith Hughes, "Walter Mosley, Socratic Method, and the Black Atlantic," in *Finding a Way Home,* ed. Brady and Maus, 38.

3. Walter Mosley, *Always Outnumbered, Always Outgunned* (New York: Norton, 1998). All parenthetical citations of the book in this chapter refer to this edition.

4. Wilson, *Walter Mosley: A Critical Companion,* 134.

5. Walter Mosley, *The Tempest Tales* (Baltimore: Black Classic, 2008). All parenthetical citations of the book in this chapter refer to this edition.

6. Harriet Jacobs, *Incidents in the Life of a Slave Girl: Written by Herself* (Boston: Published for the author, 1861), 86, *Documenting the American South,* docsouth.unc .edu/fpn/jacobs/jacobs.html (accessed March 1, 2014).

7. Review of *The Tempest Tales, Kirkus Reviews,* May 20, 2010, www.kirkusreviews .com/book-reviews/walter-mosley/the-tempest-tales/ (accessed March 1, 2014).

8. Francesca Canadé Sautman, "Devil with the Blue Eyes: Reclaiming the Human against Pure Evil in Walter Mosley's *The Man in My Basement,*" in *Finding a Way Home,* ed. Brady and Maus, 45.

9. Walter Mosley, *The Man in My Basement* (New York: Back Bay, 2005). All parenthetical citations of the book in this chapter refer to this edition.

10. Ben Greenman, "What Lies Beneath," review of *The Man in My Basement, New Yorker,* January 19, 2004, www.newyorker.com/magazine/2004/01/19/what-lies-beneath (accessed November 1, 2014).

11. Ralph Ellison, "Working Notes on *Invisible Man*," in *The Collected Essays of Ralph Ellison,* ed. John F. Callahan and Saul Bellow (New York: Modern Library, 2003), 343.

12. Dubois, *The Souls of Black Folk,* 10–11.

13. Devika Sharma, "The Color of Prison," *Callaloo* 37 (2014): 662.

14. Walter Mosley, *The Last Days of Ptolemy Grey* (New York: Riverhead, 2011). All parenthetical citations of the book in this chapter refer to this edition.

15. Tim Rutten, review of *The Last Days of Ptolemy Grey, Los Angeles Times,* November 18, 2010, articles.latimes.com/2010/nov/18/entertainment/la-et-rutten-20101118 (accessed November 1, 2014).

16. Marilyn Stasio, "An Eye for and Eye," review of *The Last Days of Ptolemy Grey, New York Times,* November 19, 2010, www.nytimes.com/2010/11/21/books/review/Crime-t.html?partner=rss&emc=rss (accessed November 1, 2014).

Chapter Seven—Nonfiction

1. Mosley, *Life Out of Context.* All parenthetical citations of the book in this chapter refer to the Avalon 2006 edition.

2. Walter Mosley, *Workin' on the Chain Gang: Shaking Off the Dead Hand of History* (Ann Arbor: University of Michigan Press, 2000). All parenthetical citations of the book in this chapter refer to this edition.

3. Owen E. Brady and Derek C. Maus, "Introduction," in *Finding a Way Home,* ed. Brady and Maus, xv–xvi.

4. Mosley, *A Red Death.* All parenthetical citations of the book in this chapter refer to the Pocket 1992 edition.

5. W. E. B. DuBois, "Talented Tenth," in *The Negro Problem: A Series of Articles by Representative American Negros of To-Day,* ed. Booker T. Washington (New York: James Pott and Co., 1903), 33.

6. Ibid., 75.

7. Walter Mosley, *What Next: A Memoir Toward World Peace* (Baltimore: Black Classic, 2003). All parenthetical citations of the book in this chapter refer to this edition.

8. Review of *What Next: A Memoir Toward World Peace, African American Literature Book Club,* aalbc.com/reviews/whatnext.htm (accessed November 1, 2014).

9. Mosley, *Fearless Jones.* All parenthetical notes in this chapter refer to the Warner Books 2002 edition.

10. Keeanga-Yamahtta Taylor, "Abusive Relations: Democrats and Black America," review of *What Next: A Memoir Toward World Peace, International Socialist Review* 49 (September–October, 2006), isreview.org/issues/49/review-Mosley.shtml (accessed November 1, 2014).

11. Brady and Maus, "Introduction," xvi.

12. Walter Mosley, *The Man in My Basement,* (New York: Back Bay, 2005). All parenthetical citations of the book in this chapter refer to this edition.

13. DuBois, *The Souls of Black Folk.*

14. Mosley, *Twelve Steps Toward Political Revelation*. All parenthetical citations of the book in this chapter refer to the Nation 2011 edition.

15. Review of *Twelve Steps Toward Political Revelation, Publisher's Weekly,* www.publishersweekly.com/978-1-56858-642-7 (accessed November 1, 2014).

16. Review of *Twelve Steps Toward Political Revelation, Kirkus Reviews,* March 2, 2011, www.kirkusreviews.com/book-reviews/walter-mosley/twelve-steps-toward-political-revelation/ (accessed November 1, 2014).

17. Walter Mosley, *The Long Fall*. All parenthetical citations of the book in this chapter refer to the New American Library 2010 edition.

SELECTED BIBLIOGRAPHY

Easy Rawlins Series

Devil in a Blue Dress. New York: Norton, 1990. New York: Pocket, 1991.
A Red Death. New York: Norton, 1991. New York: Pocket, 1992.
White Butterfly. New York: Norton, 1992. New York: Pocket, 1993.
Black Betty. New York: Norton, 1994. New York: Pocket, 1995.
A Little Yellow Dog. New York: Norton, 1996. New York: Washington Square Press,
   2002.
Gone Fishin'. Baltimore: Black Classic, 1997. New York: Pocket, 1998.
Bad Boy Brawly Brown. Boston: Little, Brown, 2002. New York: Grand Central, 2008.
Six Easy Pieces: Easy Rawlins Stories. Boston: Little, Brown, 2003.
Little Scarlet. Boston: Little, Brown, 2004.
Cinnamon Kiss. New York: Little, Brown, 2005.
Blonde Faith. New York: Little, Brown, 2007. New York: Grand Central, 2008.
Little Green. New York: Doubleday, 2013.
Rose Gold. New York: Doubleday 2014.
Charcoal Joe. New York: Doubleday, 2016.

Fearless Jones Series

Fearless Jones. Boston: Little, Brown, 2001. New York: Warner Books, 2002.
Fear Itself. Boston: Little, Brown and Co., 2003.
Fear of the Dark. New York: Little, Brown and Co., 2006.

Leonid McGill Series

The Long Fall. New York: Riverhead, 2009.
Known to Evil. New York: Riverhead, 2010.
When the Thrill Is Gone. New York: Riverhead, 2011.
All I Did Was Shoot My Man. New York: Riverhead, 2012.
And Sometimes I Wonder About You. New York: Doubleday, 2015.

Science Fiction

Blue Light. Boston: Little, Brown, 1998.
Futureland: Nine Stories of an Imminent World. New York: Warner, 2001.
The Wave. New York: Warner, 2006.

Socrates Fortlow Series

Always Outnumbered, Always Outgunned. New York: Norton, 1998.
Walkin' the Dog. Boston: Little, Brown, 1999.
The Right Mistake. New York: Basic, 2008.

Juvenilia

47. Boston: Little, Brown, 2005.

Other Novels

RL's Dream. New York: Norton, 1995.
The Man in My Basement. Boston: Little, Brown, 2004. New York: Back Bay, 2005.
Fortunate Son. New York: Little, Brown, 2006.
The Tempest Tales. Baltimore: Black Classic, 2008.
The Last Days of Ptolemy Grey. New York: Riverhead, 2010.
Parishioner. New York: Vintage, 2012.
Debbie Doesn't Do It Anymore. New York: Doubleday, 2014.
The Further Tales of Tempest Landry. New York: Vintage, 2015.
Inside a Silver Box. New York: Tor, 2015.

Erotica

Killing Johnny Fry: A Sexistential Novel. New York: Bloomsbury, 2007.
Diablerie. New York: Bloomsbury, 2008.

Plays

The Fall of Heaven. New York: Samuel French, 2011.
Lift. Unpublished. World premiere at Crossroads Theatre Co., April 10, 2014.

Nonfiction

Workin' on the Chain Gang: Shaking Off the Dead Hand of History. New York: Ballantine, 2000.
What Next: A Memoir Toward World Peace. Baltimore: Black Classic, 2003.
Life Out of Context: Which Includes a Proposal for the Non-violent Takeover of the House of Representatives. New York: Avalon, 2006.
This Year You Write Your Novel. New York: Little Brown, 2007.
Twelve Steps Toward Political Revelation. New York: Nation, 2011.

Graphic Novel

Maximum Fantastic Four. New York: Marvel, 2005.

Crosstown to Oblivion

The Gift of Fire / On the Head of a Pin. New York: Tor Books, 2012.
Merge / Disciple. New York: Tor Books, 2012.
Stepping Stone / The Love Machine. New York: Tor Books. 2013.

Select Secondary Works

Auden, W. H. "The Guilty Vicarage: Notes on the Detective Story, by an Addict." *Harper's,* May 1948.

Berger, Roger A. "'The Black Dick': Race, Sexuality, and Discourse in the L.A. Novels of Walter Mosley." *African American Review* 31 (1997): 281–94.

Brady, Owen E., and Derek C. Maus, eds. *Finding a Way Home: A Critical Assessment of Walter Mosley's Fiction.* Jackson: University Press of Mississippi, 2008.

Bunyan, Scott. "No Order from Chaos: The Absence of Chandler's Extra-Legal Space in the Detective Fiction of Chester Himes and Walter Mosley." *Studies in the Novel* 35 (2003): 339–65.

Chandler, Raymond. "The Simple Art of Murder." In *The Longman Anthology of Detective Fiction,* ed. Deane Mansfield-Kelley and Lois Marchino. New York: Pearson, 2005. 208–19.

Crooks, Robert. "From the Far Side of the Urban Frontier: The Detective Fiction of Chester Himes and Walter Mosley." *College Literature* 22.3 (1995): 68–91.

Ford, Elisabeth A. "Miscounts, Loopholes, and Flashbacks: Strategic Evasion in Walter Mosley's Detective Fiction." *Callaloo* (2005): 1074–90.

Forter, Greg. *Murdering Masculinities: Fantasies of Gender and Violence in the American Crime Novel.* New York: New York University Press, 2000.

Gray, W. Russel. "Hard-Boiled Black Easy: Genre Conventions in *A Red Death.*" *African American Review* 38 (2004): 489–98.

Gruesser, John Cullen. "An Un-Easy Relationship: Walter Mosley's Signifyin(g) Detective and the Black Community." In *Multicultural Detective Fiction: Murder from the "Other" Side,* ed. Adrienne Johnson Gosselin, 235–55. New York: Garland, 1999.

Kennedy, Liam. "Black Noir: Race and Urban Space in Walter Mosley's Detective Fiction." In *Diversity and Detective Fiction,* ed. Kathleen Gregory Klein, 224–39. Bowling Green, OH: Bowling Green State University Popular Press, 1999.

King, Nicole. "'You Think Like You White': Questioning Race and Racial Community through the Lens of Middle-Class Desire(s)." *Novel: A Forum On Fiction* 35.2–3 (2002): 211–30.

Levecq, Christine. "Blues Poetics and Blues Politics in Walter Mosley's *RL's Dream.*" *African American Review* 38 (2004): 239–56.

Lock, Helen. "Invisible Detection: The Case of Walter Mosley." *MELUS* 26.1 (2001): 77–89.

Lomax, Sara M. "Double Agent Easy Rawlins: The Development of a Cultural Detective." *American Visions* 7.2 (1992): 32–34.

Mason, Theodore O., Jr. "Walter Mosley's Easy Rawlins: The Detective and Afro-American Fiction." *Kenyon Review* 14.4 (1992): 173–83.

Nash, William R. "'Maybe I Killed My Own Blood': Doppelgangers and the Death of Double Consciousness in Walter Mosley's *A Little Yellow Dog.*" In *Multicultural Detective Fiction: Murder from the "Other" Side,* ed. Adrienne Johnson Gosselin, 303–24. New York: Garland, 1999.

Pepper, Andrew, "'The Fire This Time': Social Protest and Racial Politics from Himes to Mosley." In *The Contemporary American Crime Novel: Race Ethnicity Gender Class.* Chicago: Fitzroy-Dearborn Press, 2001.

Reddy, Maureen T. "Race And American Crime Fiction." In *The Cambridge Companion to American Crime Fiction,* ed. Catherine Ross Nickerson, 135–47. New York: Cambridge, 2010.

Saunders, Charles R. "Why Blacks Should Read (and Write) Science Fiction." In *Dark Matter: A Century of Speculative Fiction from the African Diaspora,* ed. Sheree R. Thomas, 398–404. New York: Aspect, 2000.

Sharma, Devika. "The Color of Prison." *Callaloo* 37 (2014): 662.

Smith, David L. "Walter Mosley's Blue Light: (Double Consciousness) Squared." *Extrapolation* 42.1 (2001): 7–26.

Soitos, Stephen F. *The Blues Detective: A Study of African American Detective Fiction.* Amherst: University of Massachusetts Press, 1996.

Stein, Thomas Michael. "The Ethnic Vision in Walter Mosley's Crime Fiction." *Amerikastudien / American Studies* 39 (1994): 197–212.

Wesley, Marilyn C. "Power and Knowledge in Walter Mosley's *Devil in a Blue Dress.*" *African American Review* 35.1 (2001): 103–16.

Wilson, Charles E. *Walter Mosley: A Critical Companion.* Santa Barbara, CA: Greenwood, 2003.

Young, Mary. "Walter Mosley, Detective Fiction and Black Culture." *Journal of Popular Culture* 32.1 (1998): 141–51.

INDEX